P9-APH-469

Susan Greenberg

Love & Memory

Love & Memory

a novel by Amy Oleson

spinsters book company
SAN FRANCISCO

Copyright © 1991 by Amy Oleson. All rights reserved

First edition.
10-9-8-7-6-5-4-3-2-1

Spinsters Book Company
P.O. Box 410687
San Francisco, CA 94141

Cover art by Kathryn Roake
Cover and text design by Pamela Wilson Design Studio
Copy editing by Kathleen Wilkinson
Production by: Jennifer Bennett   Liz Broderson
                  Margaret Livingston   Aron Morgan
                  Pamela Ai Lin To   Meredith Wood
Typeset by Joan Meyers in ITC Galliard

Printed in the U.S.A. on acid-free paper.

All persons represented herein are fictional. Any similarity to persons living or dead is a coincidence.

Library of Congress Cataloging in Publication Data

Oleson, Amy, 1956-
     Love and memory: a novel / by Amy Oleson. —1st ed.
          p.   cm.
     ISBN 0-933216-85-8 : $9.95
     I. Title
PS3565.L443L6 1991
813'.54—dc20

                                              91-214292
                                                   CIP

Acknowledgments

Many women have contributed to this book. Thanks to everyone who read it along the way.

Special thanks to—
My mother, for raising me to believe anything's possible; to Martha Lipshitz, for being there when this all began; and to Bonnie, Janet, and the rest of the Wild Women, scattered now far and wide.

Carol Martin, you made one of the hardest parts so easy. Thank you.

Sometimes it seems there are certain people whom fate never intended for you to meet and then by the strangest quirks of chance you meet them anyway—or, as my dad might have said, sometimes you just get lucky—Sue Cobb, the Denver chamber of commerce never had a better spokeswoman. (Okay, so it doesn't just snow in the mountains...)

And to the rest of the bunchagirls—Kate Shea, Karen Henry, C.L., Georgiann (Fatty) Sanborn, Barb Horn, Cooie Kenyon, Mo—thanks for sharing the good times.

For Sharon, who made this possible in so many ways.

Chapter One

Liz Edwards glanced at her watch as she ran across the last intersection and turned towards home. Exhilaration surged inside her as she glimpsed the flashing numbers—her time was excellent. She had just passed forty minutes and she was nearly home.

One block to go, hold on, she ordered silently. Her legs responded with long, even strides. Liz ignored her fatigue and the aching in her lungs. Glancing closely enough at the cracked and uneven sidewalk to avoid tripping, she eyed the distant corner and urged her body into an all-out sprint.

Liz slowed to an easy jog when she reached her house; she stopped at the steps leading to the yard. Bent over, chest heaving, the sound of a facetious whistle and three distinct claps reached her ears. Liz did not rush to look up.

"A stellar performance this morning, ladies and gentle-women, right here in Watertown, Massachusetts, by every-one's favorite dark horse, Elizabeth Edwards! Ms. Edwards has just shattered the nine-minute mile! And they said it couldn't be done. Care to say a few words to your adoring fans, Ms. Edwards?"

Liz had partially regained the ability to breathe normally. She stood up and gave her roommate Alice the benefit of her sardonic smile. "What in the world are you doing up so early?" she asked.

"I don't know, what time is it?"

3

Liz looked at her watch. "Nine-fifteen."

"How far'd you run?"

"Five miles. And closer to eight-minute miles, thanks just the same."

Alice whistled. "You are taking this getting-in-shape stuff seriously."

Liz walked into the yard. Alice sat on the steps of the dingy gray three-decker house in which they shared a first-floor apartment. In the last nine months Liz had learned to forgive the shabby exterior of the old house. Not that theirs was any more run-down looking than the other houses on the street; the inside, remodeled several years ago, more than compensated for the house's outward flaws.

Liz resisted the impulse to join Alice. Instead, she leaned over and began stretching the backs of her legs. "This summer I am going to be in shape," she called out. "You think you're the tough one. Just wait. Pretty soon you'll be chasing me in soccer or football, or whatever other sport we end up playing."

She rambled on. Alice made some reply but Liz did not acknowledge it. Next thing Liz knew, Alice was on top of her. Caught off guard, she fell easily to the ground beneath Alice's weight.

"How about wrestling?" Alice asked. "Think you can beat me there?" She struggled for Liz's arms, her intent clearly to pin her.

"Not fair," Liz gasped as she tried to roll away. "I just finished running. Give me a break."

"Nope. You're the one who wants to be in shape. Think of this as my contribution to your training."

Alice grabbed one arm. Liz swung the other free. Alice straddled Liz at her hips and leaned forward to reach for her flailing right arm. Liz grunted and tried to squirm away; but Alice had had the advantage from the beginning, and she had arms and legs far stronger than Liz's own, the product of hours spent lifting weights. Liz knew her cause was hopeless. All she wanted was to prolong the struggle one, maybe two, minutes more.

"Didn't you have a date last night?" she asked, grimacing as she barely evaded being pinned.

"Yep. She wouldn't let me stay all night. Said her mother was coming over for breakfast."

"And you believed her?"

Alice paused to stare straight down. "What do you mean?"

Liz took advantage of Alice's distraction. Summoning all of her strength, in one motion she tried to lift Alice and roll away. Alice caught the movement and held her back. Afterwards, neither spoke.

Liz had only managed to get on her side while Alice remained on top of her. Now Alice used the weight of her lower body to roll Liz backwards. She grabbed and held Liz's left wrist; seconds later she trapped her right wrist. The match was over. Liz reluctantly looked up to see Alice looming over her.

"You know, Edwards," Alice said, gasping between breaths, "if you weren't certifiably insane, you and I could have a great life together."

Liz, more winded than Alice and still in the vulnerable position of having her arms held, was undaunted. "Ha! Some life it'd be for me, you gone five nights out of seven, flexing your muscles to impress every sweet young thing who shows up at the bar. Sounds terrific."

"Hmm," Alice said in nonreply. She released Liz and brushed perspiration from her brow. Liz looked at the damp, dark curls on Alice's forehead and took some consolation in knowing that Alice had worked up a small sweat. She rolled away and began rubbing her wrists.

"I guess we'd better get going," Alice said.

"Going? Where?"

"Soccer practice. Ten o'clock this morning. You wondered why I was up."

"I didn't know we had practice today. I'd never have gone running. When did you find out?"

"Last night. Jeanne called. She found out yesterday we can use the field at Magazine Beach in Cambridge today and next Saturday. I left you a note. I guess you didn't see it."

"Oh god! I'm going to die out there."

"I know," Alice agreed, chuckling. "I can't wait to see it."

———

Three long hours later Liz sprawled on the grass near her soccer bag. She stared across the field to the river, too tired to move. A rare speedboat brightened the murky brown-green of the Charles; sleekly crafted rowing sculls were a far more common sight on the water. Liz watched the boat until it disappeared beneath a bridge; then she lay flat on the grass,

5

indulging in a last moment of rest before Alice or somebody would tell her she had to stand up. Across the river, she saw the Prudential and the Hancock tower dwarfing the other buildings of the Boston skyline.

At a nearby restaurant Liz straggled after her teammates and sank into a padded seat against the back wall. "My first real day of vacation, almost my last, and I feel terrible," she exclaimed to no one in particular.

Alice had taken the chair across from her. "Liz," she said, "it's Saturday. Most people don't consider Saturday a vacation day."

"Great. Then this year I don't get any."

"Are you taking classes this summer, Liz?" Randi, who was sitting next to her, asked.

"No. I'm off until fall. But I have to work a regular job for the summer as part of my program. I start on Monday at Allied Industries."

"Are you working downtown?"

"No. I'm at their corporate information center out in Concord."

A waitress came by to take drink orders.

"Good practice today," Jeanne, their team captain, said after the waitress returned with two pitchers of water. "Everyone looked awfully good."

"I'll say," Alice agreed. "Suzanne's friend, the blonde, looked great."

Liz groaned.

"What's the matter, Edwards?" Alice asked.

"Oh, it's just that some things never change. I should be used to that by now."

"I guess you're right, some things never do. Speaking of which, have a date for tonight?" Alice taunted.

Liz rolled her eyes then turned to accept the glass of water Randi passed to her.

"One question," Jeanne said loudly, attempting to get the attention of the eight women seated. "I need to know what everyone wants to do about our roster size. We have fifteen women from last year. There are four or five who would like to join the team. I know some of you think twenty is too many. Personally, I think fifteen is too few. Any thoughts?"

A buzz of conversation sounded around the table when Jeanne stopped. Liz tried to think through the dilemma but her brain, exhausted from the previous week of final exams,

6

refused to engage. She leaned her head into the corner and instead thought how much she liked Jeanne. Without changing position she shifted her eyes and saw Jeanne's head nodding, apparently in enthusiastic agreement with something Mary had said. Her short blonde hair bobbed with the motion of her head; her smile was easy and unaffected. Jeanne was attractive, no question, but Liz thought she was also the most compassionate, fair-minded, intelligent woman she knew. Jeanne was single this summer, Liz mused, letting her eyes linger another moment.

The talk continued among the women around her. Liz closed her eyes and smiled as fragments of conversation reached her ears.

Alice kicked her under the table. "What are you thinking, smiley?"

Liz opened her eyes. "Oh, just that everyone will say her piece and then we'll do exactly as Jeanne proposes, which is add the new players to the roster, but tell them they might not play much at first. By mid-season people will be injured or on vacation and we'll need the extra bodies."

"Oh Liz, do you always have to be the wise observer?"

Liz opened her eyes wider. "Not just an observer. No, Alice, I know you don't believe me, but this is my summer for action."

Alice started to protest.

"No, no, I'm serious. School is over, it's summer, the weather is going to be great, and I'm ready to have a good time!"

Alice's brown eyes flashed in obvious disbelief. "And I'm to believe that includes romantic pursuits?"

"You'd better believe it."

Alice smirked. "When I see it."

Their waitress returned to take food orders. Liz ordered a salad, recalling how poorly she had eaten this whole last week.

"What excitement is on your agenda for today?" Alice asked later, after several in their group had left.

"I think I've had it. I'm exhausted."

"Ah Liz, I thought you just told me you were changing your ways. I should have known that was only so much talk."

Liz reluctantly opened her eyes and tried to stare down her roommate. "Alice," she said, "it is nearly the end of May. This is the very first day since last September that I haven't had a single thing to do. I was thinking of driving to the coast of Maine. I guess I'll have to go tomorrow, though I know that hardly qualifies as excitement in your book. I suppose I could rush out and have my hair tinted Day-Glo green as evidence of my changing life, but to tell you the truth, my clothes just wouldn't match. So, you will just have to be patient, but I promise you, you will see changes. I—"

Alice interrupted. "Liz, I get the point." She paused and frowned. "Day-Glo green? Nah, I don't think that's your color at all."

"All right, then, I'll marry a woman who has green hair."

"That's a fine plan. As long as you're willing to date women who have brown, or blonde, or red hair."

Liz glanced down the table. Jeanne had her wallet out and had pushed her chair back; she seemed to be getting ready to leave.

Blonde hair, Liz thought, amused at her impulse to check.

❀

Monday morning, Liz sat alone in the Human Resources office of Allied Industries. That obnoxious man, Jim, or Tim, had disappeared ten minutes ago. Liz glanced at her watch. It was ten-thirty. She had arrived at eight this morning and so far had done nothing but fill out one meaningless form after another. Now Jim—Jim Wright, Liz saw, turning to read the name on the door—had gone in search of yet another.

"This is exactly what I hate about big companies," she muttered softly.

Allied Industries had not been her choice for the summer internship assignment. Liz's brow furrowed as she wondered again how she had ended up here. Six weeks ago she and her classmates had had to submit names of companies where they wanted to work for the summer. Liz had submitted three, any of which would have been fine. But to have been assigned to Allied Industries—she kicked the wooden desk in front of her in deepening frustration. It just didn't make sense. No one else in her program had been denied all of his or her choices, no one she knew of, anyway. One of her classmates, a former Allied employee, had assured her she would find the work here deadly dull.

Liz broke off from her thoughts to smile. She reminded herself that by the time internships had been announced, she hadn't cared very much where she was assigned. Two weeks earlier she had had a letter from the department telling her she had won one of BU's academic excellence awards. Liz smiled wider. The ten thousand dollar tuition scholarship was going to go a long way towards keeping her out of debt.

"Here it is," Jim called out in false cheer as he re-entered the office. "Sign this, then I'll take you to your new department."

"What is it?" Liz asked as she reached for the paper.

"Your promise that you won't disclose any of what you learn about our business to our competitors. And, that you will leave behind all of your work when your internship is over. Finally, that Allied retains the patents or copyrights to anything you may produce while you're here."

Liz snorted quietly and took the paper from his hand. It was a lousy deal, but it was also a lousy three-month job. She signed the page and pushed it across the desk.

"I guess that's it," Jim said. "Now the fun starts. You'll be working in the Materials/Finance Department, reporting to Glenn Kiley. Follow me and I'll show you to your summer home." He stood up and Liz happily did the same.

In a distant section of the building Jim stopped outside of one cubicle. "Well then, here we are," he said. "Liz, I would like you to meet Laura Jansson. Laura is Glenn's second-in-command. Laura, this is Liz Edwards. She'll be your student intern for the summer."

Laura, a small woman whom Liz guessed to be in her early thirties, stood staring wide-eyed at them both. Finally she said, "There must be some mistake. I had no idea we were having an intern in this department. I don't think Glenn knows either."

"I don't know anything about that," Jim said. "I do know that Bob Jenkins was the one who assigned Liz here."

Bob Jenkins, Liz recalled, was the head of the Northeastern Regional Accounting Division.

To Liz he said, "I'm sorry. I didn't tell you that Glenn is on vacation. Laura will handle your assignments for the remainder of the week. I'm sure you can use the time to settle in."

Turning to Laura on his way out, he said, "If there's anything else you need to know, check with Bob's secretary. They have all of the details there."

Liz and Laura stood at the office door, an awkward silence between them. Finally Laura said, "Please, come in. Have a seat."

Both women sat down but Laura remained quiet. Liz stole a closer look at her. Laura's hair was dark blonde, long and unstyled with straight bangs across her forehead. She was dressed casually, wearing a short-sleeve striped blouse tucked into a plain light blue skirt. Liz appreciated what she thought was a sense of carelessness in Laura's attitude towards her appearance.

"I'm sorry," Laura said, "I don't mean to be rude. It's just that I'm a little taken aback that you're here. I had no idea you were expected."

"Is there a problem? I've known about this assignment for two weeks."

Laura laughed shortly. "That figures. I wish communication around here were half as prompt. Tell me Liz, what is your background in computers?"

Liz began to describe the graduate program she was enrolled in as well as the two jobs she had held before returning to school. As she spoke, she felt irritated to realize she was speaking as if she needed to prove her qualifications. She hadn't wanted to come here in the first place; she certainly did not have to defend her right to be here. Afterwards, she tried to phrase her words more matter-of-factly. Laura smiled and listened politely, but Liz was further annoyed by the feeling that Laura's thoughts were elsewhere.

When Liz finished, Laura proceeded to offer an overview of the Materials/Finance Department. The anger Liz had felt towards her moments earlier began to fade. Laura warmed up to the conversation. Liz was surprised when she glanced at her watch to see that an hour had passed while they talked.

"Well, we certainly got off the track, didn't we?" Laura said.

"Only a little," Liz agreed. "What kind of work do you think I'll be doing here?"

Laura frowned. "I really can't say right now. I'll have to think about that. Why don't I show you to an office you can use for now, and in a little while I'll introduce you to the others."

Laura walked with Liz to an office a few doors down the corridor. Liz noticed that her office, a cubicle similar to Laura's, was directly opposite the secretary's desk. Behind the secretary's desk was an office with real walls and windows. The plate on the door showed the name: Glenn Kiley.

Inside her cubicle Liz found the familiar items of a modern, modular office: a desk, a chair, and a computer terminal sitting on a stand adjacent to the desk. A set of manuals, their covers torn and pages ripped out then jammed carelessly back in, stood slumped against each other on a shelf above the desk. Liz reached for one and sat down to read.

Two days later, she was still reading the manuals. Liz paced restlessly inside her small space after a futile attempt to concentrate. The manuals didn't make a bit of sense. She was more than ready to have real work to do.

Liz sank heavily into her chair and wondered whether Laura would show up today. Yesterday—Tuesday—she hadn't seen her at all.

"I'm having a little trouble thinking of something for you to do," Laura had said on Monday, the last Liz had seen of her. "Why don't you read the manuals—"

Liz felt the muscles on her forehead crease in a frown. This department was bizarre. Oh, the people seemed nice enough, even Laura. But every single person she had met so far had acted as if she had just stepped off another planet when she told them she was a student intern.

"Does Glenn know about this?" Donna, the department's secretary, had asked at lunch that first day. Still the same old story, Liz thought in disgust—the loyal female assistant protecting the empire of the male boss. Fortunately, she would only be a peon in this particular empire for three months.

But you can't kill time without injuring eternity. Liz grinned and quickly recovered her good humor, remembering Thoreau's famous words. She had stopped to walk at Walden Pond on her way home from work last night. After getting home she had been inspired to leaf through Alice's copy of *Walden and Civil Disobedience* and had recognized that line and other well-known passages.

What would Henry David think about the high-tech hysteria that has swept New England, Liz wondered, ignoring the open manual on her desk. She could guess the answer— that he would despise everything about the machines and the overdevelopment they had brought to this quaint country land.

Liz looked up in surprise when she heard light tapping. Laura was standing in her doorway.

"Hi," she said. "Listen, Liz, do you have plans for lunch today?"

"No."

"Well, would it be all right with you if you and I go out? I'd like to talk to you and I'd just as soon do it away from here."

There was an unmistakable urgency in Laura's voice. Liz looked at her curiously. "Sure, we can go wherever you want to."

Laura's smile was apologetic. "Sorry. I don't mean to be cryptic. I'll explain everything later."

Liz speculated on Laura's odd invitation all morning. Finally it was twelve o'clock. She and Laura left the building and drove to a nearby restaurant.

"There's something I have to tell you," Laura said after they had ordered, "but I'm not sure what to say or where to begin. So, maybe if you just hear me out, you can ask questions later and I can clarify whatever's confusing."

"Okay," Liz answered nervously.

Laura took a deep breath. "I feel like you've been put in an awkward, unfair situation and I'm not sure how it's all going to work out. I'm sure it's no secret to you that everyone in Materials/Finance was shocked at your arrival the other day. Well, the truth is, none of us expected to see an intern in this department ever again. We had an intern last summer, someone also from your school, who ended up causing quite a lot of trouble. His name was Eric Redmond. Have you heard of him?"

Liz shook her head no.

"To make a very long and ugly story short," Laura continued, "Eric did not work out very well. He intentionally changed the data in several areas prior to a major system update which in turn caused massive damage to our permanent records and data files. What you have to understand, Liz, is that our systems are old and decrepit. When this happened last summer, it was more than a catastrophe. We were in the process of compiling quarterly reports for our plant managers. Of course they were all furious—first, that we gave them reports with incorrect figures, then second, that it took so long to get everything fixed. Glenn took a horrible amount of abuse through it all, which, though not surprising, never seemed fair.

"It was a terrible time for everyone, but especially for Glenn. The situation was so serious that Bob Jenkins threatened to fire her. As it turned out, she wasn't fired. Still, it took a long time for things to get back to normal. Our department always has been looked down upon a bit by the other departments. This only helped to lower our reputation even further."

Laura paused. "I guess what I'm trying to say is that I don't understand how you managed to get placed with us. Glenn made it clear a long time ago that she never wanted to see another intern in her department. The fact that you started here on her first day of vacation makes me wonder whether Bob Jenkins isn't playing some kind of game with her. If that's the case, then I truly am appalled that you are being used in this way. But Liz, please understand, I'm only speculating. I'm not kept very well informed of departmental politics.

"Anyway, that, unfortunately, is the situation. Glenn will be back on Monday. I have no idea what she'll do. Anything could happen." Laura frowned and sipped unhappily from her water glass.

Liz was shocked. In her wildest dreams she could not have imagined herself involved in the situation Laura had just described. Yet here she was, feeling as if she were little more than a pawn.

Suddenly a question occurred to her. "Glenn Kiley is a woman?" she asked. "I assumed Glenn was the name of a man."

Laura laughed. "Of course she is. I thought you knew that."

Liz shook her head no.

"You know," Laura continued, "it is possible that I've blown this thing out of proportion. Glenn may be thrilled to have another person around to help with the work. We do have a lot backlogged right now. I don't know. I can't begin to make any sense of it all."

"Now I understand," Liz said, thinking of why she had had no work since she'd arrived.

"I didn't know what to tell you, Liz. I've been a little confused about my loyalties. I like you. I think you're bright and I know you can do our work. But I also know Glenn and I don't think she's going to be happy about this."

Laura continued to appear agitated even after she stopped speaking. She brushed at something on her blouse sleeve;

then she glanced around at the people sitting nearby, as though worried someone might have overheard her.

"It sounds like what happened last year was hard on you, too," Liz said quietly.

"Yes, it was."

Liz almost regretted having said anything. Laura's gaze became unfocused and for a long moment she was silent.

"Do you get along well with Glenn?" Liz asked, struggling to keep their conversation alive.

Laura gave a short laugh. "Yes, we work very well together."

Liz feared another period of silence, but with revived energy Laura continued, "Glenn changed last summer. She seemed very angry for a long time. I don't know if she was upset about work or if it was something else. As much as I like Glenn, we are not friends. Glenn keeps her distance from people at work. Even so, it used to be that she would join us at lunch or after work for a drink once in a while. Now she never does. I suppose I miss it that she doesn't."

Liz sensed Laura's feelings for Glenn were strong. Though she tried to imagine what Glenn was like, no image came to mind.

"The thing with Glenn," Laura went on, "is that you never know what she's going to do or how she's going to react. We could sit here all day wondering, but neither of us will know anything until Monday morning."

Liz nodded. She thanked Laura for being honest with her. They finished lunch and returned to work. Although Laura had not said as much, Liz knew that the decision as to her work assignments would come only from Glenn, and therefore not for several more days. She groaned as she picked up another boring, barely decipherable manual.

❁

Inside her bedroom Liz stacked her neatly folded clothes on the bed. An open suitcase lay nearby. Silently, she marked off the collected items against a checklist in her mind. Liz looked up as Alice entered.

"Everything ready for your trip?" Alice asked.

"Almost." Liz picked up a floral print dress. "I hate this dress my sister picked. I'm not even in the wedding. You'd think I could choose my own dress."

Alice laughed. "What time does your plane leave?"

"Two, I think." Liz chuckled sarcastically. "At least I don't need to ask anyone's permission to leave work early tomorrow."

"Your boss comes back on Monday?"

"That's what Laura says."

Alice walked over to Liz's bed. She sat on the end for a few seconds, then stretched her long lanky frame out on the space Liz was not using. She stared at the ceiling and said, "Hmm, a woman manager. This could be interesting."

Liz went to her closet and scanned its contents. "Let's hope it's not," she said as she picked out another blouse.

"So, are you looking forward to this wedding?" Alice asked.

"No. Yes. I'll be glad to get it over with. Oh, I forgot to tell you—you're going to love this. Two weeks ago Judy called and asked if I wanted to bring Chris to the wedding. Chris! Can you believe it?"

Alice sat up. "Your sister never knew about your relationship with Chris, did she?"

"No. I never talked to her about it anyway. But Judy's asked about Chris before. So what do you think," Liz asked, pausing to grin. "Is Judy on to me?"

"Sounds like she might be. What did you say about the wedding?"

"Oh, just that I hadn't seen Chris for a while and that I definitely would not be bringing her to the wedding."

Alice resumed her former position, reclining on Liz's bed. She said, "I only talked to Chris once, that time she called last Christmas. She was drunk. Charming personality."

"She thought you were my lover. Actually, that's the last time I spoke to her, too. Thanks just the same but that's fine with me." Liz placed the last of her piled clothes into the suitcase and closed the lid.

"You're not still stuck on that relationship, are you, Liz?"

Liz shrank from the concern she heard in Alice's voice. "No. I'm not. Why do you ask?"

Alice shrugged. "Just wondered."

Liz lifted the suitcase from the bed and turned towards the door of her room. She frowned, trusting that Alice could not see her face. Over the last year, especially during the previous fall and winter, she had told Alice the story of her botched relationship with Chris. Not willingly. Alice had forced the issue, questioning her time and time again. Liz had grown sick of that conversation long before Alice ever had. But it had been good to talk; Liz knew that now. Fortunately— finally—that part of her life was behind her.

"Hey, I've got an idea," Alice said. She sat up. "Take me to the wedding with you. Tell Judy we can make it a double ceremony. Think of it, Liz, that's one way to tell your parents you're a dyke."

Liz gave Alice what she hoped was her most winning smile. "Sorry Alice. Plane's full. In fact all flights to Buffalo tomorrow are booked. I think we'll just have to do it another time."

Chapter Two

As Glenn Kiley stepped out of her office, intending to drop a folder on Donna's desk, she saw a dark-haired stranger enter the vacant office across the hall.

"Hello," she called. "Who are you, and what do you think you're doing in there?"

"I—I'm Liz Edwards. I've been assigned here on a summer internship."

Glenn stared at her in a cold fury that had sprung to life in one instant. "No, you've got that wrong," she countered slowly and deliberately. "Now I would appreciate it very much if you would leave here, go back to whoever sent you, and tell that person he or she has made a mistake."

"Glenn, hello." Glenn turned to see Laura rushing up the hall. "I see you and Liz have met."

"Laura, you know about this?" she asked, motioning slightly towards Liz.

"I didn't. Last week someone in Human Resources brought Liz here. Her assignment was coordinated through Bob's office."

"Laura, come into my office, please."

Inside her office Glenn stood momentarily at the window on the far wall. Early morning sunlight sparkled on the tree just beyond the glass panes, the tree she had watched growing through the seasons in each of the last three years. Glenn sighed heavily.

Laura was already sitting down. Glenn frowned, sensing Laura's anxiety across the space that divided them. She turned around. "All right, tell me what happened. From the beginning," she said in a voice devoid of emotion.

Laura described the events of the previous week, including an account of her phone call to Bob Jenkins' secretary to verify the fact that Liz was supposed to be in the department. Everyone had assured her that Liz was in the right place.

"What have you had her do?" Glenn asked when Laura finished.

"Nothing. Glenn, I knew you didn't want an intern here. I've just had her read the old manuals."

"Thanks." Glenn almost smiled. "I appreciate your handling it that way. I suppose I'll have to have it out with Bob to get her moved out of here. That should be a lot of fun."

Glenn paused to gaze at the opened and unopened mail which Donna had left on her desk.

Laura stood up. "Oh, how was your vacation?"

Glenn did smile now. "It was nice, thanks."

Laura nodded and turned to leave.

"Laura, stop back a little later this morning, okay?" Glenn said. Her voice had softened considerably. "I'll want to hear about the rest of the week. Any other surprises I should know about?"

Laura laughed. "No. Other than Liz's arrival it was a very normal week. I'll see you later, Glenn."

After Laura left, Glenn sorted through the stack of folders on her desk, looking for the latest reports on component shipments. She needed to get ready for tomorrow's meeting with the plant managers. Anticipating that, already she felt tense. This month, as usual, she would no doubt be blamed for providing insufficient data for effective materials management.

Or else she was tense about Liz Edwards.

Glenn dropped the folder she was holding. Another student—what a sick joke. She glanced at her watch: it wasn't yet nine. Too early for Bob. For a split second she wondered whether she even wanted to confront Bob over this situation. In two weeks she would be gone. One phone call, that's all she waited for; then she planned to tell Bob exactly what he could do with his students—and this job. She was leaving Allied Industries, and at this point it couldn't happen soon enough.

On the other hand, Glenn thought—beginning to feel almost philosophical—since she was leaving anyway, what did she care if she risked a major blow up?

———

"Glenn, hello," Bob greeted when Glenn appeared in his doorway. "Come on in. How was your vacation?"

"Fine. Bob, why did you assign a student intern to my department without telling me?" Glenn walked in and sat down, scowling for once at the juvenile collection of golf trophies Bob kept on the shelf behind his desk.

"Oh, you're referring to Liz Edwards, aren't you? Arrangements were made ten days ago, or so. I was over at Ashbury for two days, then you went on vacation. It was an oversight that you weren't told. Why? Is there some problem?"

Glenn stared intently at him, unsure whether he was telling the truth. She quickly decided that didn't matter. "Yes, there's a problem. I don't want her. You'll have to find some other department that will take her."

"Glenn, don't get so upset. It's only for the summer."

"I won't take her! I made it clear a long time ago that I would never have anyone in my department whom I hadn't hired."

"You're referring to our Mr. Redmond of last year, I see. This is not the same situation at all. Liz Edwards is here on the highest recommendation from her professors. She's just about the best they have over there."

"I don't care. I don't care if her father is president of MIT and her mother chairman of the board at Digital Equipment. I won't take her!"

"That's too bad, because you're stuck with her."

"Why?" Glenn demanded furiously.

"Look, everyone was upset about what happened last year. The university is as anxious to set things right as we are to maintain a good relationship with them. It's a mutually dependent relationship," he added evasively.

"But why my department?"

"Why?" Bob repeated. "I'll tell you why. It's because you have an empty office. No other department manager does."

The simplicity of this explanation stunned Glenn. She stood up and walked behind her chair to the window and said, "Do you want to hear something completely ridiculous? I believe you." She shook her head and gave a short laugh. No other department had the space because they were fully staffed, but every request she had made in the last six months to hire another person had been denied.

"I'm not going to cooperate with you on this, Bob."

"I'm sorry, but it's settled. Liz Edwards is your responsibility until the end of the summer, or until another office opens up, whichever comes first."

"No, it is not settled," Glenn returned. "I may have to live with her presence in my area, but I promise you, I will not give her one bit of work to do."

Bob shrugged and said, "You're the manager."

❈

Liz was completely exasperated. Not one thing had happened all day. Nothing had happened, no one had even spoken to her since early that morning except Donna, Glenn's secretary, who greeted her as she went in and out of her office.

You'd think I had the plague, she whispered softly, staring vacantly at the slate-colored fabric of her cubicle wall.

Liz spun in her chair angrily, tense with frustration. She glanced at her phone and at the number of the computer science department she had scribbled down, but she didn't call. Be patient, she told herself, repeating the advice she expected to hear if she did call school—let Allied management work this out. Somebody would have to work something out. It was clear she could not work with Glenn Kiley this summer.

"Bitch," she swore softly.

The next morning Liz sat restlessly at her desk waiting for something to happen. Something did. Laura appeared in her doorway.

"Hi. Long day yesterday?" Laura asked.

Liz rolled her eyes and nodded. Before she could say anything, Laura said, "I have to go and talk to Glenn now. I assume something's been decided about you, although I have no idea what that is. I'll let you know when I hear."

Liz heard the sound of Glenn's door closing as Laura went in. Less than five minutes later, Laura reappeared. Liz saw the downcast expression on her face and felt afraid before Laura said one word.

"Can you meet me for lunch today?" Laura said.

"Sure. What—"

"Sorry, Liz. I'll have to tell you what's going on then."

The morning hours dragged by, until at noon Liz escaped.

"Liz, I really don't know what to say," Laura began. They were seated in the same restaurant where they had eaten nearly a week before. "Glenn tried to have you transferred out of the department but failed. Now she says she isn't going to give you any work to do. I can't begin to guess what's going on."

"What do you mean she's not going to give me any work?"

"Just that. She talked to Bob Jenkins yesterday. He won't move you."

Liz stared disbelievingly; gradually Laura's words sank in. Glenn would have her sit there all summer without one bit of work or responsibility. Liz tried to speak but only choked soundlessly on her words.

"Who knows?" Laura continued. "This all could change tomorrow. I'm really sorry, Liz. I'm sorry that we're both caught in the middle of such adolescent behavior."

Hearing this, Liz couldn't help but smile. It was the most severe pronouncement she had ever heard Laura utter. "I appreciate your telling me, anyway," she said. "To be honest, I never expected it to work out this badly. Is there anyone else I could talk to? Bob Jenkins, maybe?"

Laura shook her head. "Bob wouldn't be any help to you. If I know Glenn, she made it perfectly clear to him what she intended to do. No, the only thing you could do is go back to someone at your school and explain what's happening. Even then, I'm not sure what you could accomplish."

"Or I could quit the internship," Liz said softly.

"Yes, you could do that. I'm sure Glenn is hoping you will."

Liz felt a surge of new anger. "Well, I'm not going to quit. If I don't complete an internship this summer, I won't get my degree in the spring!"

"I know. Maybe if you just try and hang in there for a while, who knows, things might change. I'll do what I can to help you, Liz, but right now my hands are completely tied."

Liz returned unwillingly to the office which, in the space of one hour, had become her prison. All afternoon she struggled to contain her fury. Outwardly, she appeared calm; inside, she seethed.

Every seven or eight minutes she reached for the phone, determined to call school. What would anyone there say about this? Each time she restrained herself from actually making the call. She wanted to think this through carefully—and maybe find a way to handle it on her own—before she appealed to someone in the department to intervene.

It seemed all too clear what was going on now. She had been offered to Allied Industries as a token from the university. It was up to her to correct the tarnished image the school had suffered by Eric Redmond's actions last year. That was why she had been denied her own internship requests. And what would happen if she walked out of this one now? Would the department withdraw her scholarship? Did she even care?

Liz glared at the walls until five o'clock arrived. She walked angrily from the building and on the way home stopped at a used bookstore. She bought six books for five dollars and stored them all in the glove compartment of her car. Unless by some miracle Glenn graciously permitted her to work, tomorrow, Liz decided, she would read.

❊

Glenn sat behind her closed office door staring absently at the familiar objects in the room: the impressionist prints on the far wall; the two chairs opposite her desk; her single plant, suffering from want of attention, on top of the file cabinet in the corner. In the last hour she had accomplished nothing.

Oh, there was no shortage of work to be done. She glanced at the neatly collected reports waiting for her review. The reports showed the results of system problems recently fixed. Unfortunately, that stack was far shorter than the ever-growing stack of new problems reported. It was, and always had been, a losing battle to keep pace.

Glenn wondered whether she even liked her job. What a ridiculous question. Hadn't she just spent the entire previous week extolling the satisfaction she took in managing computer operations? Her vacation last week had been no vacation. The real reason she had traveled to San Francisco had been to interview for a new job.

At twenty minutes until quitting time, Glenn officially abandoned working for the day and turned in her swivel chair to gaze through her window.

It wasn't work that she disliked, Glenn reminded herself. This particular job was her problem. Long before today the excitement had gone out of it. She hated her job; she hated the rest of her life—moving would free her of both. Glenn thought about her plans to pack everything she owned and move three thousand miles away from all of the people she had ever loved. Her stomach muscles tightened in fear as the reality of what she was about to do swept over her. But that just didn't matter. Rather, it didn't matter enough. She had to move.

"But why California? Why now?" Pamela, her best friend, had asked at dinner the night before.

Glenn frowned at the memory of their conversation. Pamela had known of her plans for more than a month. Now that this move was about to happen, Pamela had become fiercely antagonistic. Glenn heard her questions again. Why did she have to move? Why, of all places, to California? Oh, Pamela had always asked more questions than anyone else, Glenn thought, laughing derisively. But this had become too much. Better than anyone, Pamela ought to understand why moving was exactly what she had to do.

Glenn exhaled a tired sigh and turned to shut and lock her desk. Time to go home and spend another evening waiting for the phone call that would give her her ticket out of this place.

Her phone was ringing when she opened her front door. It stopped before she was two steps inside. Glenn felt her anxiety swelling when five minutes passed and the phone didn't ring again. She debated calling the firm in San Francisco, assuring herself her inquiry would not be inappropriate. Fifteen long minutes later the phone finally rang again. Glenn answered it, nevertheless tensing when she recognized the voice of the woman at the consulting firm where she had interviewed.

"I'm glad to have finally reached you," the woman said. "I want to thank you again for making the trip west. I hope you enjoyed your week in San Francisco."

"I did. Very much," Glenn replied, concealing the impatience in her voice.

"I want to reiterate, as I hope I expressed to you when you were here, how happy I am at your interest in our company and what a good addition you would be to the North Point Consulting Group."

"Thank you."

"With that said I must tell you, Glenn, that I definitely want to offer you a job, but I'm unable to do so right now."

Glenn's heart sank. "Why? What happened?"

"You understand, of course, that we're a consulting company and that we must sell our services. We have a particular client that does a great deal of work with us. They have a project that has been delayed. So the position I had in mind for you did not open this week. I trust them when they say the delay is only temporary."

"How long? How long do you think it will be?"

"Roughly, six weeks."

"Six weeks!"

"I'm sorry, Glenn. Six weeks is not a very long time. It is possible something else will open before then and if it does, I will contact you immediately."

Glenn struggled to keep emotion out of her voice. "And what if nothing does open? Are you telling me there'll be no job?"

"That's unlikely. The economy is doing very well in the Bay Area and our services are widely used. If by some fluke this position does not materialize, something else will. I want to hire you, Glenn, I hope I've made that clear. However, you are under no obligation to us and if you choose to take another position, unfortunately, that will be our loss."

Glenn's eyes were blazing when she hung up the phone. Six weeks—she wanted to start packing this instant! Oh, she had had other interviews; there were positions at other companies she could pursue. But this was the job she wanted.

"Six weeks is not a very long time," the woman had said.

For whom, Glenn thought miserably. For her, six weeks seemed an eternity.

❋

Liz read three books in three days hardly stirring from her cubicle and at the same time managed to write long tortured letters full of self-pity to her good friend Jennette who lived in Philadelphia. Friday afternoon, she reread her latest letter. Liz scowled then shredded it as she had all the others.

"Come with me to my softball game tonight," Alice said when Liz got home from work that evening.

Liz glanced up from the kitchen counter where she stood leafing through the assortment of junk mail that had arrived that day. "Where are you playing?"

"South Boston."

24

"Great. It's the start of a summer weekend and you want to go anywhere south of the city? You'll be stuck in traffic headed for the Cape for hours. Anyway, isn't South Boston the team you fought with after the tournament last summer?"

Alice walked over to the stereo and removed a record from the turntable. Liz laughed to see the holes showing at the top of Alice's worn socks; she admired, as usual, the sight of Alice's lean body.

"Oh, come with me," Alice said. "You can run for help if things get out of hand."

Liz decided she had absolutely nothing better to do. She changed into shorts and a t-shirt and sat down on the couch to tie her sneakers. "What's Carol doing tonight?" she asked.

"Working late. She was going to come to the game. We're meeting at the bar later."

"How long have you been seeing her? Two weeks? This must be serious, Alice."

Alice's small face became wrinkled in an expression of false hurt. "It is love, my friend, and I am in such a good mood I'm not even going to return your heartless jab regarding the longevity of my love affairs. Let's go. I'll show you some back streets you never dreamed existed."

The summer wind was warm as it blew in off of the salt marshes east of the softball field. Liz didn't know many of Alice's teammates, and she was not terribly interested in this game. After two uneventful innings had passed, she gave up watching altogether and lay down on the rough wooden bleachers. When Alice's team came off the field for their turn at bat, Liz sat up. Minutes later, when they returned to the field, she moved higher in the empty stands and lay down again, hearing, just barely, sounds on the field.

"Get a hit, babe, you're a hitter."

"Play's at first, nobody out."

There was a lull while the ball was being pitched, then Liz heard the dull thud of the bat smacking, a hit heading somewhere into the field.

"Way to go, Alice. Great catch," someone on the defense called out.

Liz smiled. She knew of no sport in which Alice did not excel. Alice was a gifted athlete, and she took her sports seriously. Not fanatically, the way Mary on their soccer team did, yelling at people when they made mistakes. Alice just played well and always had a good time.

Overhead, white fluffy clouds mixed in constantly varying shapes. Liz watched them and hardly noticed when her eyes closed. The team came in from the field but nobody climbed the bleachers to where she lay. All sounds seemed to blend into one. Liz wondered, as she had throughout the week, what she would do about her job. She had fallen into an impossible situation. Glenn was a bitch: that's what Kathy Green, one of the department's systems analysts, had said. A great looking bitch, but a bitch. Liz imagined Glenn off with some handsome man, waltzing around with him as if he were some damned show piece, bending her body underneath his because that's what women like her were supposed to do with men. Glenn Kiley might have risen to a position of some power but along the way she had sold her soul. In the haze of her half-thoughts Liz swore to herself that no matter what was at stake, she'd never do the same.

"I'm glad you found the game so exciting."

Alice's words stirred Liz out of her light sleep; she sat up. Just as she regained an upright position she was startled to feel Alice, who was sitting behind her, begin rubbing her shoulders.

"Nice bed you've chosen. Jesus, Liz, your shoulders are tight."

"It's that hard work I've been doing all week," Liz replied, still groggy, but awake enough to feel confused at how much she wanted Alice to touch her. Alice massaged her back and shoulders; then she reached to her neck and into her scalp. Liz groaned at the soreness in her body. Though she feigned nonchalance, in reality, her senses were reeling.

"Guess we should get going," Alice said, breaking the contact at the same moment Liz warned herself not to let this go on.

Liz stood quickly. She extended her leg to the next seat and stepped down. "No fights after this game?" she asked without looking back.

"No. They brought us beer as a peace offering. Want some?"

"Sure." Liz rushed down the bleachers towards the open cooler at the bottom. Alice followed. Liz handed one can to Alice and opened the other for herself, carefully avoiding eye contact with Alice.

While Alice stopped to talk to one of her teammates, Liz stared across the playing field towards the eastern horizon.

Get hold of yourself, she whispered in silent warning. She glanced over her shoulder to look at Alice. Alice looked unbelievably attractive, wearing that silly baseball cap, her shoulders exposed now that she had removed her game shirt and wore only a tanktop underneath. Liz took a second swallow and tried to remember how many times this had happened before—five? six? This was not the first time she had felt intensely attracted to Alice.

"Ready to go?" Alice called. Liz nodded and began walking towards the parking lot.

Inside the car Liz struggled to make small talk. "Seems hard to imagine, but this time last week I was home for the wedding," she said.

"Did something at the wedding upset you?"

"No. Nothing in particular. I already told you all of the highlights. Why?"

"You seem quiet. I wondered."

"Oh, no. I was just thinking about work during the game. I don't know what I'm going to do about my job."

Liz turned to look through the side window as they drove through the congested streets of Dorchester, the old wood frame three-decker houses built so close they were practically touching one another. Alice's thoughts were still with the game. Liz listened to her stream of comments closely enough to reply in monosyllables when necessary. Her own thoughts were vastly different.

Is it purely arrogance, she wondered, that makes me think I need only give Alice some small sign and she would stay with me—would sleep with me—tonight?

At home Liz opened a second beer. She ignored for the moment the grumbling in her stomach and sat down to watch the Red Sox on TV. Alice showered, then got ready to leave. Liz felt torn between an anxiousness for her to be gone and disappointment that Alice seemed so oblivious of her. Then when the door slammed behind Alice, Liz grew angry at the mocking stillness she left behind.

Hours later, alone in her bed, Liz was powerless before the image of her body's desire to have Alice come to her as she had once before, to take her in her arms, strip her clothes and take her to bed. All she wanted was to have Alice hold her in her strong arms and love her, for Alice to touch her, to grip her body and lay open the deep recesses she chose to keep hidden.

Wide awake in the darkness, Liz didn't know if it made her feel better or worse to think this might still be Alice's fantasy, too.

❋

When Miriam called on Thursday to invite her to go away for the weekend, Glenn didn't hesitate to accept. Desire to see Miriam was only part of her quick decision—perhaps the smaller part, she admitted, slightly guiltily. Going away was the draw; escaping the questioning eyes of her friends, a close second. Wanting to spend time with Miriam came somewhere after both.

Miriam, at forty, was ten years older. Glenn wasn't bothered by their age difference. It was something else that seemed to go with it, the sense she sometimes had that Miriam saw herself as wiser and more experienced—her feeling that Miriam occasionally felt the need to try to take care of her— that she resisted. Glenn doubted, once Miriam heard her news, that that would be a problem this weekend.

"It wasn't exactly a sudden decision," Glenn said, driving west on Route 2. She was glad to have the distraction of driving as a buffer against Miriam's disappointment.

"I'm sure it wasn't," Miriam responded, subdued. "Tell me more."

At first, the idea of moving had been a lark, a fantasy, Glenn explained. For too long she had felt her life had stalled in important ways and she had begun exploring ideas for possible new adventures. As a wild fantasy, she had dreamed of moving to Australia to live and work for a few years. Then she had had the idea of moving to San Francisco. It, too, had been a fantasy, until sometime in late spring when gradually she became more serious about it.

As she told of her week in San Francisco, her anticipated job offer, and the delay, Glenn glanced sideways at Miriam. Miriam was attractive—dark, her features angular. Her world was academia; she was an associate professor of sociology at Boston College. Through the early months of last winter she and Miriam had enjoyed an intense—but brief—romance. Glenn knew that her feelings had changed, not Miriam's, but they had parted on good terms and still dated on occasion. Glenn was surprised to realize she hadn't seen Miriam in nearly two months.

They stopped for dinner in Deerfield. While they were eating Miriam seemed to recover from her disappointment.

"How is Pamela?" she asked over a last cup of coffee. "I haven't seen her since Marie and Eve's spring party."

"She's fine. As are Diana and Joyce."

"And I presume they are less than thrilled by your plans to move?"

"That's right."

After dinner they drove the rest of the way into the Berkshires and found their cottage. The cabin was small and rustic, but the view from the front window, a rolling meadow leading to green foothills, visible even in the fading light, moved both Glenn and Miriam to forgive the shortcomings of their accommodations. Miriam shut and locked the door. She walked to where Glenn stood in the middle of the room. Glenn felt a moment's hesitation, but when Miriam leaned forward to kiss her, she returned the kiss.

"I'm glad you decided to come with me," Miriam said when she moved back. She lifted her hand to Glenn's cheek.

"I'm glad you called."

Glenn followed Miriam into the bedroom. She fell heavily on the bed and lay flat on her stomach.

"Rough week?" Miriam asked. She moved close to Glenn and began rubbing her back.

"Very rough. This feels wonderful."

Glenn felt Miriam using both hands to massage her. Miriam rubbed deep into her neck and back; occasionally, the fingers of one hand slipped to her side, lightly teasing her breast. Glenn felt herself quickly becoming aroused. Then Miriam reached underneath her, moving her hand from her breast to her stomach. Glenn rolled over.

"And how was your week? How is your class going?" she asked, already feeling flushed and wanting to prolong the sensation.

"Very well. I only have a few students this summer. I'm enjoying them."

Glenn knew from past encounters that Miriam would probably want to talk about her work. She did. Glenn closed her eyes and listened while Miriam described her research and her hopes for getting new grant money.

"It's always hard when you move to a new place," Miriam said, returning to their earlier conversation. "And there are always unexpected gains and losses."

29

Glenn's eyes opened. "What do you mean?"

"Oh, just that when you make a decision such as the one you're about to make, you think you know what you're giving up and what you'll get instead. What you can't predict is how you're going to change and how the people in your life will change, too."

"I guess that's part of the risk."

"It is. On the other hand, simply staying in one place is no guarantee against change either. We both know that."

Glenn nodded.

"Oh, come on, we don't have to talk about this," Miriam said. "We'll both end up depressed."

Glenn guessed what Miriam would propose instead. She wasn't wrong. Miriam's gentle caresses became unmistakably more seductive. In public, Miriam seemed very much the conservative, sedate scholar she was, although it had been many years since she had exerted any effort towards concealing her sexuality from her colleagues. In private, her bearing was much different. Miriam became deeply sensual. Glenn had always been attracted by Miriam's sexual uninhibitedness.

Miriam rolled on to her side, the fingers of one hand trailing beneath Glenn's light shirt. Glenn smiled at the contact. She felt a growing excitement as Miriam moved slowly towards her breast. Still, when Miriam's fingers actually brushed across her nipple, Glenn inhaled sharply. Miriam hesitated; Glenn smiled quickly to reassure her.

Inside, Glenn felt a raw hunger spring to life. She was startled by the urgency of her desire to be touched. By Miriam. Maybe by anyone. Tonight Miriam would undress her, then she would begin kissing her, and she would kiss her all over until Glenn felt weak with sated pleasure. For one hour, or two, she would have the luxury of forgetting all the problems in her life.

Miriam lifted Glenn's shirt to her neck; Glenn raised her head and Miriam pulled it away. Then Miriam loosened the top of Glenn's pants. Glenn shuddered as she felt Miriam's cool fingers stroking her skin. She closed her eyes and breathed deeply while Miriam traced the curves of her body. Then Miriam nudged her over. Glenn rolled to one side, lifting her hips; Miriam slipped the pants off.

Without warning, the sensual mood was broken.

"Glenn, you're so thin!" Miriam gasped.

Frowning, Glenn looked down the length of her body, seeking proof for this accusation.

"I don't believe you," Miriam continued. She reached over to touch Glenn's stomach. Her hands moved to Glenn's shoulders, then to her legs. There was nothing seductive in her touch now.

"Were you trying to lose weight?" she asked.

Glenn started to turn away. Miriam quickly reached over to prevent her. "No, of course I wasn't trying," she answered moodily.

Miriam's hand was on her stomach feeling where her hip bone jutted out. She spoke softly. "You've always been thin, Glenn, but this seems a little extreme."

Glenn sighed unhappily. "You're right. I guess this whole question of moving has made me a little anxious. It's hard to make myself eat when I don't feel hungry."

Miriam leaned over and drew Glenn into her arms. She kissed her and stroked her gently. "Well, I suppose this just means we get to eat all we want to this weekend."

Glenn forced her smile and her reply. "That might be a good thing," she agreed.

Hours later, after they had made love, after Miriam had fallen asleep, Glenn lay awake at her side. She gazed towards the ceiling, which in the darkness she could not see. A weight of depression filled her. She was almost, but not quite, sorry she was here with Miriam. Being here was still better than being alone.

But was it, she wondered bitterly. Glenn felt tears in her eyes. She had chosen to come here so she wouldn't have to see her own friends. Why? How had that happened?

This last year had been so unbearably hard. Not just that she and Diana had broken up—yes, just that she and Diana had broken up, Glenn admitted angrily, angry that after a year of living without Diana, she still felt so raw and hurt.

Not always. Oh, yes, she and Diana had both gone on—Diana to Joyce and she to other women—dating again, doing what she had to do to go on. When would life get easier, Glenn demanded, hardening herself against futile emotion. When she moved?

She tensed, then held herself still, careful not to wake Miriam.

But the voice inside her head would not be silenced.

She had tried. This whole last year she had really tried to hold herself together, to make the best of something for herself. Nothing had changed. Nothing was any better. Had she fooled anyone? Was she fooling Diana or Pam now, or did they know she had already started pulling away?

Her quiet tears fell as Glenn thought of Pamela and Diana, even Joyce—thought that wherever she had drifted to, whatever her problems had become, those three were no longer able to help her. Miriam was right. Things change even if you stay in the same place.

Chapter Three

"I saw you talking to Jeanne before the game tonight," Alice said to Liz when they returned home after Monday night's game.

Liz opened the closet door and tossed in her soccer bag. Alice walked over to add hers.

"Yes. I told Jeanne about my screwy problem at work. I was hoping she could make some sense of it all."

"And?"

"She couldn't. She said I probably got caught in the middle of something and it was entirely possible Glenn Kiley intended to ignore me all summer. Her only suggestion was that I make up some project of my own to work on. Ha!"

Liz sat down on the couch. She unlaced and removed her shoes then placed both feet on the worn coffee table. Alice fell into their comfortable, old recliner from the side, leaving both legs dangling over the chair's arm.

More tentatively, Alice asked, "Has Jeanne said anything else to you recently?"

Liz felt herself flush. She lowered her head to escape Alice's observation. "Yes. Tonight she did. Why?"

"What did she say?"

"It sounds like you already know! Do you?"

"Know what?"

Liz looked suspiciously at her roommate. "Jeanne asked me out."

"So what did you say?"

Liz braced herself against Alice's disapproval. "I told her I didn't think it was such a great idea. I don't know," she added weakly, "I think it's better if Jeanne and I stay friends."

"Edwards, I don't know about you!" Alice said, giving full vent to the criticism Liz had anticipated. "For the last five months all you have ever said about dating anyone is that you think Jeanne is attractive. The woman asks you out and what do you do? You immediately crawl under your same old rock! Jesus! Nice vacuum you have; lived here long?"

"I'm not enjoying this."

"Well, phew! That makes two of us."

"Alice, leave me alone. I don't need this. In case you haven't noticed, my life is not in such great shape." Liz stood up, intending to retreat to her room. Mid-stride, she changed her mind and instead sat down on the floor and began stretching.

Liz bent one leg back and leaned towards her other knee, stretching the back of her leg. Her long hair fell forward covering her face. Liz heard Alice adjust the recliner and lie back. An uneasy silence filled the room.

"Did you tell Jeanne to ask me out?" Liz asked abruptly.

"I'm not in the habit of telling Jeanne who to date."

Liz paused to glare at Alice, half in disbelief, half in anger.

"Look, Jeanne did tell me she was thinking of asking you out," Alice admitted. "That's all. I didn't say anything. Silly me, I thought you'd be thrilled to go out with her."

"I did what I thought was best, can't you accept that?"

Alice stared hard at her. "No, Liz, I can't. You have everything going for you. You're smart and you're attractive and you're even a half-decent soccer player. Don't pretend you don't know other women on the team have been interested in you. And for god's sake, don't tell me again about that little affair you had with Eileen last summer. Jeanne—"

"It wouldn't work, I know that!" Liz interrupted, angrier now. "Even Jeanne says she's not ready to get involved with anyone. What would be the point? I just know it wouldn't work."

"You don't know any such thing. All you know is that you won't try. You're not dealing with reality, Liz. You're dealing with your own screwed up version of life and the world and women."

"Oh, and you're supposed to be some kind of expert?"

"No, I'm no expert. But at least I feel my feelings, and I take my chances, and, do you know, I even make love with other women once in a while!"

"I didn't start this conversation," Liz said testily. "And if you don't mind I'd like to end it now." She stood up and started for the hall that led to her bedroom.

"Liz," Alice called plaintively, "will you at least think about going out with Jeanne?"

It was not a good night for sleeping. Liz tossed and turned fitfully through the first hours of the night. Past 1 a.m. she switched on her light and started reading. Not for one moment did she allow herself to think about Alice.

Sometime towards morning she fell asleep. Sometime after that her consciousness was overtaken by the too vivid images of her dreams.

Liz became aware of raindrops falling. She sensed the motion of a car. A slow horror grew in her as she realized where she was: she was in that car. She could feel the steering wheel in her hands; she saw, in the darkness, misty splashes on the windshield.

In her nightmarish reality the voice was speaking, that twisted, mutant voice which she knew was some part of her own. "You're a fool, Liz," it whined, "everyone knows it. So Chris has left you again? You just thought you didn't want her."

"I do not want her!" Liz screamed in response. "I don't want anything!"

"Oh? Then why are you so upset?"

Liz slammed her foot to the gas pedal.

The signs flashed by overhead. Liz sped beneath one that showed the name Syracuse and an arrow pointing in the direction of the highway. In minutes she was on unfamiliar country roads.

It wasn't a dream, it was happening. Liz saw the wet road in front of her. The road was poorly lit but it appeared to be slick. She didn't care. Her only thought was to escape. To escape Chris—to escape her own awful life. To escape that hated voice, which even now taunted mercilessly.

"You're a fool, Liz. You have no capacity to act," it repeated.

"I don't care! I don't care!" Liz screamed. "I just don't care," she whispered.

She pressed the accelerator hard, braking rapidly when she approached a curve. Every muscle in her body had tensed. Liz kept her eyes glued to the road surface. She drove on a long straight stretch; then she was at the bend. Still she did not attempt to slow the car. Rounding the curve she saw—as she knew she would—the other car, that damn car! It had pulled onto the road and it had stopped.

Beneath the sheet her foot strained powerfully against the nonexistent brake. Her effort was to no avail. In her mind Liz saw the pavement which safely separated the two cars vanishing rapidly.

Liz sat bolt upright, breathing hard. For several seconds she stared at the far wall. Images sorted slowly. The rainy night. Early morning light. She glanced at her nightstand and saw the picture of Jennette and Louise next to the red digits of her clock radio. She was in Boston—this was Boston. Still shaken, she released her arms and fell back on her bed.

But she hadn't hit the other car, she reminded herself, as if that was necessary. She had avoided it by forcing her own car off the road. Her car had slid off the shoulder and had rolled over, turning over completely, only coming to rest when the passenger side had lodged against a tree. Miraculously, she had walked away from the wreck with only cuts and bruises. No one had ever known how fast she had been traveling just before the accident, nor her own frame of mind at the time.

Liz felt her breathing slowly become more regular. This time it had been six months since she had had the dream.

———

Laura wasn't in that morning; Glenn didn't seem to be around either. Liz knew not one soul would enter her office. She threw paper clips at her walls and let her useless thoughts run wild.

Moving 320 miles hadn't changed a thing. Chris was still with her. Sixteen months they had lived together—not exactly an eternity, Liz thought. Yet those months, and the five she had spent living alone in Syracuse after the breakup, marked a turning point in her life, a downward turn, apparently still going down—her life still bound to Chris. It didn't matter that she was in Boston. It didn't matter that she had lived here for more than a year.

Liz looked at her hands, enfolded on her lap, folded into each other, just as she was folded into herself. She laughed shortly. Alice had told her once she had nice hands. Long, slender fingers, Alice had said; she liked that in a woman. Liz felt tears spring to her eyes. Would she ever make love to a woman again?

She had been bluffing all those times when she said she was attracted to Jeanne. Yes, she did think Jeanne was attractive —but no, she didn't want to go out with her! She didn't want to go out with anyone. She had nothing to give. Hadn't she proved that last year with Eileen, only going out with her to please Jennette? Liz stiffened at the memory of the conversations she had had to force, at how she had resisted Eileen's tenderness, feeling dead inside, just dead.

It only made her feel worse, knowing she hadn't always felt this way. This barrenness was Chris's legacy to her.

Angrily, Liz wiped her swollen eyes, wondering whom she hated more: Chris, for accepting her love falsely, knowing she had no love to return; or herself, for having had to flirt so closely with death before she found the strength to walk away.

At noon Liz phoned Jeanne. Unexpected pleasure surged inside her when Jeanne said she'd love to get together for dinner that night.

They met at an Italian restaurant in the North End. Liz crossed the floor to where Jeanne sat at a table by the window, forgetting her frustration at having spent the last ten minutes driving the narrow, winding, brick streets searching for a parking spot. Red-checkered table cloths and empty chianti bottles, short candles jutting from the top and melted wax hardened on the sides, decorated each table. Between the pungent smell of garlic and the doughy aroma of fresh bread, the voices speaking Italian—or English with heavy accents— Liz felt as if she had entered another world.

Liz had feared she might be nervous, but her anxiety faded after Jeanne admitted she wasn't seeking a romantic involvement.

"I didn't think I was in love with Charlotte, but I'm having a hard time dealing with our separation," Jeanne said, referring to the woman with whom she had broken up earlier in the spring. "I enjoy spending time with you, Liz, but I don't want to mislead you. I'm really not ready to get involved in another relationship. I hope I haven't offended you."

"You haven't. Thanks for being honest." Liz laughed before adding, "Now I don't have to be nervous."

Jeanne raised her eyebrows mischievously. "Don't get too relaxed. Someday I might want to make you nervous."

After they finished dinner Jeanne looked at her watch. "It's two-for-one night at the bar. I don't feel like doing a lot of drinking, but there might be a good crowd. Feel like going?"

"Sure. For a little while."

Only a few women were seated around the bar when Liz and Jeanne entered the building; likewise, most of the tables were vacant.

"Maybe we'll see Alice and Carol here tonight," Liz said as they sat down.

"Maybe so. Those two have been spending a lot of time together lately."

"They've been going out for more than three weeks. I think that must be a new world record for Alice."

Jeanne offered to get their drinks. She returned with two glasses of beer.

"I'm glad we talked earlier," Liz said when Jeanne sat down, "but Alice will be disappointed if we don't indulge in a hot and heavy romance. I think she stays awake at night trying to figure out how to get us together."

"Alice thinks the answer for everyone is to be in love. Maybe that is the answer for her." Jeanne started to say something else but stopped. Her eyes were on the bar. Liz took a sip from her glass and was about to turn her head to see what Jeanne was looking at. Jeanne spoke in a rush.

"Liz, wait. In just a minute I want you to look to your left, towards the bar. Okay, now."

Liz followed Jeanne's instructions and turned her head surreptitiously. Her eyes scanned the bar. Suddenly everything inside her froze.

"Oh, she's looked away now," Jeanne said. "Did you see her? She certainly was looking at you."

Liz's heart was pounding hard and her eyes were locked on the table top.

Jeanne repeated her question.

"That was Glenn!" Liz whispered in a hiss. "Glenn, from work!"

"Oh my," Jeanne said. "She's very attractive, Liz. And she's a dyke. That's great!"

Liz waited a few seconds then pushed her chair back from the table and stood up. "I have to go," she said.

Jeanne looked at the bar. "No you don't. It looks like your boss has already left."

"I have to leave."

Liz rushed from the room. She was on the sidewalk before Jeanne caught up with her.

"Liz, what's wrong? Your boss is a lesbian. Now she knows you are, too. What's the big deal? Maybe she'll come to her senses and treat you with some respect."

Liz stopped and spoke in a short, clipped tone. "Because I'm a lesbian? Because we're both gay?"

"No, of course not. But this does give you a new common ground. It might be all Glenn needs to change her attitude towards you."

"I don't want preferential treatment because of my sexuality!" Liz exclaimed, laughing derisively. "I'd settle for ordinary treatment. Anyway, who knows what she was doing in there? She certainly wouldn't be the first straight woman to step foot in there."

Liz's heart was pounding violently as she resumed her rapid pace down the street. All she wanted was to find her own car and get away.

"Liz, wait. I don't get it. Why are you so upset?" Jeanne called from behind.

Liz ignored her. She rushed along the sidewalk and didn't stop until Jeanne called out again. Turning, she almost spoke viciously. "I hate her, Jeanne. I really do. I didn't know that until I saw her just now. I wanted so much from this summer and she's ruining it all!"

Jeanne reached out for her. Liz resisted, but gave up struggling when she felt Jeanne's arms around her. Suddenly, everything just seemed too hard. Liz felt tears rising behind her closed eyes.

"All I want is to work on equal terms with the others in that department," she exclaimed, embarrassed by the few tears that had escaped. "I'm twenty-seven years old, I'm not a child! I know a lot about computers, Jeanne, I really do. I know I can do their work." Furiously, Liz wiped her eyes.

"I believe you, Liz. I know you're smart. You couldn't have survived a year of BU's program, let alone win a scholarship, if that wasn't true. Look, my car's up here. Let's get in."

Liz yielded to Jeanne's direction. Inside, Jeanne slid across the seat to hold her again.

"Oh, I can't stand this!" Liz exclaimed as she shuddered violently.

"Stand what?"

"I have worked so hard trying to get my life together. Moving to Boston, meeting all of you, playing soccer, going back to school—I really thought things were going okay. Not great, mind you, but okay. Now the walls are closing in again. It was just a big joke, my thinking I could live differently, thinking I could get what I want."

Anger seemed almost to calm her. "Do you know what the truth is?" Liz continued in a hard voice. "The truth is it's better never to want any damn thing at all!"

Jeanne began shaking her. "No way, Liz. I won't take that from you. Walk away from this job. Nothing matters that much, especially not a lousy scholarship. You matter more. You have to decide what happens. Leave the damn job. Or stay. But whatever you do, make sure you do it on your own terms. Will you promise me you'll do that?"

Liz shook her head weakly. She gave her word to Jeanne, too shaken to do or say anything else.

❦

"Hey baby, think you can put that book away and take a break?"

Liz turned around, grinning, when she heard Laura's deep-throated, suggestive invitation. "For you," she stretched her arms behind her head and interrupted herself with a yawn, "I'll make time in my busy schedule."

Glenn was gone for the day. Liz knew this just as she knew so much else about what went on in the department: all day she overheard the conversations that took place at Donna's desk, just outside her cubicle.

"Don't you ever worry about getting in trouble with Glenn for having lunch with me?" Liz asked after she and Laura had gone through the food line and were sitting down.

"What's she going to do—fire me? I don't think so. Besides, having lunch with you is my own measly protest against what I consider a really lousy decision."

"Oh, I see. So I'm a cause for you. It's not that you enjoy the pleasure of my cheerful company," Liz teased.

Laura paused before taking a bite of salad. Her eyebrows knitted in exasperation beneath her straight blonde bangs. "It is decidedly the latter. Now that you mention it, you have been awfully sunny lately. What's up?"

Liz admitted that despite Glenn's failure to take her seriously, she was taking her own situation seriously. "I've been rereading the manuals. I'm sure it's no news to you that they're terrible. So, I've started trying to rewrite them."

Liz was confused by the pained expression she saw on Laura's face. "What is it?" she asked.

"Actually, we do have new manuals," Laura said, now sheepish. "If I had known you were really going to try to learn something about the department, I'd have given them to you sooner. Honestly, Liz, I don't know how you're managing to stick it out here!"

"Do you think I could still see them?" Liz asked, pretending not to notice Laura's flushed face.

"Well, sure. I wouldn't want anyone else to know that I had given them to you, though."

When they returned to the department, Laura stacked three oversized binders in Liz's arms. "There is a fourth, but I use it all the time. Let me know when you're finished with these and I'll give it to you."

Liz winked conspiratorially. "I'll get a coded message to you. We'll set up a secret meeting for the exchange."

Laura tensed visibly. "I know you're just kidding, Liz, but I could get in trouble for this. I'm going to have to work with Glenn for a long time after you're gone."

Liz hastily assured Laura she wouldn't mention the manuals to anyone. She went to her office and spent the rest of the afternoon absorbed with her reading.

"So much for my brilliant idea of rewriting the manuals," she whispered, past four-thirty, closing the first of the books. This one, at least, described clearly the year-end and the quarterly closing processes. Inventory systems and their corresponding financial reports—blah, Liz thought, almost glad not to have to touch such boring systems.

"Hey, Liz, how are you doing?" David, one of the programmers, was passing her cubicle as Liz stepped out to leave.

"Things are terrific. Busy day, as usual," Liz replied, unable to suppress her sarcasm. She was sick of people in the department being friendly when Glenn wasn't around, and ignoring her when Glenn was.

"Taking all that work home? That's quite a load," she said in a friendlier tone, pointing to the armful of printouts David carried. It was not David, she reminded herself, who had created the air of hostility around her.

"Nah, just dumping them. Hold on a minute." Liz watched as David turned down one hallway and dropped the pages into the recycling bin. She had seen others in the department tossing pages there for weeks.

"So, how are you keeping your sanity around here?" David asked when he rejoined her.

"I don't know that I had all that much to start with," Liz said lightly.

At the end of the hallway, she stopped. "David, I forgot something in my office. I have to go back. I'll see you tomorrow." She turned quickly, hoping David would not offer to wait.

"Sure. See you tomorrow, Liz."

In the department Liz easily identified David's program listings in the recycling bin. She took them, hiding them in her desk drawer along with Laura's manuals. Maybe they'd be no help at all, she thought as she switched off her office light for the second time that night. But reading program code could not be any more boring than reading manuals.

Glenn was back the next morning. Liz heard her and Donna talking about the meeting Glenn had attended the day before. Glenn's voice sounded kind; it almost always did when she was talking to Donna or Laura. Glenn, Liz gathered, had given Donna flowers, thanking her for the work she had done for yesterday's meeting.

Liz frowned, wishing she could just ignore Glenn. Hating her hadn't worked—though she had tried to for several days after seeing her at the bar. Lately, she always seemed to know when Glenn was around and who was talking with her.

Laura joined Glenn and Donna. Glenn finished her story. "Laura," she said, "if you have a minute now, I'd like to talk to you about a new report I think we can give the plant managers."

A new idea, Liz thought miserably—that's what I need. She reached into her desk drawer and took out the first of David's programs. She gazed hopelessly at the jumbled mass of arcane code, desperate to find something there to work on.

———

Liz stared at the typed letter until she had read every word. She checked her impulse to crinkle the page into a teeny, tiny ball and hurl it across the living room.

"It doesn't say one thing here about the tuition award being contingent upon anything," she said angrily to Alice. Yet that day, someone at BU's Computer Science Department had assured her that satisfactory completion of all first-year requirements, including a summer internship, was a condition of her scholarship.

"We all have our prices, Liz. Looks like free tuition is yours."

Liz scowled and replaced her letter in the envelope. She looked over at Alice who appeared all too relaxed, stretched full length on the sofa.

"Do you know what I did today?" Liz asked. "I read program code. Bad program code. Do you have any idea how boring that is? But I did it. And do you know what, Alice? After eight hours of unscrambling pure jibberish, I actually understood what that program is supposed to do!"

Liz paced until she stood near a chair. She was too upset to sit down.

"I thought you were going to rewrite their manuals," Alice said.

"I was. When I told Laura what I was doing she told me they already have new manuals. Turns out Glenn wrote them. Believe it or not, her manuals actually make sense. Okay, so maybe I was wrong," she said in false conciliation, "maybe Glenn's not a complete dolt. I guess she's only a partial dolt."

Alice chuckled.

"This is beginning to remind me of exactly how I felt in my first job, back in Syracuse," Liz continued, still heated.

"I thought Chris was your only problem then."

"She was my biggest problem. On top of that I was working my first real job. I worked for this asshole. This guy would never give me any work. He never trusted me. I had this one assignment, and for about six months all I did was redo it. Oh, it drove me nuts!"

"So what happened?" Alice asked, more interested now.

Liz shrugged. "Nothing. Not one thing. I kept trying to get somebody's attention but nobody cared. Then there was Chris always saying, 'Why are you complaining? You make good money—more than I'll ever make.' As if it was my fault she was making next to nothing at the university!" Liz turned away and looked for something to kick. She spotted Alice's tennis shoes but restrained herself from rearing back and booting them down the hallway. Instead she said, "I am sick and tired of hearing people say, 'Don't rock the boat, you don't have a problem in the world.' I tell you, I'm sick of it!"

Alice burst out laughing.

"What are you laughing at?"

"Nothing."

"Tell me," Liz insisted.

"Oh, it's just that you're so cute when you're mad."

Liz stared at Alice, stung speechless. She slammed the envelope on the coffee table and stormed out of the room.

Alice followed her. "Liz, I'm sorry. I'm really sorry. I was just trying to be funny."

Liz was lying on her bed, face down. She heard Alice enter the room then felt her moving onto the bed beside her.

"I really am sorry," Alice repeated.

Liz gripped the thin pillow beneath her. She pressed her head harder, wishing the darkness would consume her.

Alice began rubbing her back. Liz felt Alice coaxing her to roll over. Finally she did. When Alice saw the tears in her eyes, she reached across her to the nightstand for a tissue.

"Hey, I've got an idea," Alice said. "Let's go get ice cream. I'll buy." She sat up and extended one hand.

Liz smiled weakly and held hers out. "Alice, what's the penalty for murder in this state?"

Alice grinned. "Thinking of doing Glenn in?"

Liz nodded.

"In that case I think you'll get a special citation for putting her out of everyone's misery."

———

A new idea, a new idea, Liz whispered to herself the next morning. She glanced over the few notes she had made on David's programs then paused to listen to the sounds outside her doorway, wondering why she always waited until it was quiet before she left her office.

Another cup of coffee and a muffin for a late breakfast— at least the cafeteria served decent food, she thought, crossing a hallway and leaving the department quickly. Down the stairs, she pushed through the double doors and entered the next corridor. She froze when she saw Glenn in the distance, approaching her.

Glenn was alone. Liz forced herself to continue walking at an even pace. She knew, long before they reached each other, that Glenn intended not to speak to her. Liz lowered her eyes; but as soon as Glenn passed by, she whirled around, shocking herself, and watched Glenn walk away. Glenn never looked back. After the door closed behind her, Liz turned and walked on, bypassing the cafeteria, leaving the building and heading for her car.

It was warm inside the sun-baked car. Liz slouched behind the wheel and listened to the mournful tune playing on the radio. How am I supposed to live without you, Laura Branigan wailed. Liz had known, almost as soon as she reached her car, that she wasn't going anywhere. False start. I'm best at false starts, she thought disgustedly.

Liz stared out the front window, unconcerned whether anyone could see her. Probably they couldn't. Wasn't she just a ghost? Glenn didn't seem to have any problem not seeing her.

And how exactly do you see her, she asked herself absently. Glenn's image was suddenly sharp in her mind: her dancer's body, thin and lithe, yet exuding power, or strength. Or maybe that was just the effect of the tailored suits she always wore; her hair, medium brown, curling loosely just to her neck but a few stray curls always falling across her forehead; and her eyes, such a deep, clear blue—crystalline, Liz thought, though she had only ever seen them up close once, the one time Glenn had talked to her, the day she had returned from vacation.

At least now you know, Liz thought, understanding too well her recent obsession with Glenn—stunned to realize she felt attracted to Glenn.

———

"I have a couple of questions for you," Liz said to Laura at lunch that day, surprising them both by the urgency of her words.

"Well, sure, ask away," Laura said, startled, but apparently not put off.

Liz smiled apologetically. "Sorry. I just wanted to ask you about the quarterly closing. I always hear people complaining about it. I've been reading the manuals and I don't get it. It looks like a fairly straightforward process. What exactly is the problem with it?"

"Oh, is that all?" Laura asked, lightly sarcastic. "The problem is simple: it takes too long to run. Beginning to end, you're guaranteed six to eight hours processing time and that's assuming nothing goes wrong. It usually turns into a two-day affair. Believe me, you don't want to be around for that."

"So why does it take so long to run?"

"Because we're using an old, slow machine, that's why," Laura said in a tone of exaggerated patience, as if the answer were self-evident. "Our data files are massive. The programs are monsters. By the time everything gets loaded into memory, it grinds to a halt."

"Wait." Liz felt her heart leap, but she warned herself not to get too excited. "Are you saying you load in all of the data files at once? Why do you do that?"

"That's the way it's done. The data has to be there for the programs to run."

Liz nodded. She affected an easy laugh. "Okay, one last question. Who works on the programs for the quarterly closing? Is there one person assigned to it?"

"God, yes. Andrea's been stuck with it for the last year."

Liz smiled. Already she saw herself going through the recycling bin, or else sneaking into Andrea's office to find old listings—Allied's own Sherlock Holmes.

"Anything else you want to know?" Laura asked.

"Not at the moment," Liz said, casually shaking her head no.

ChapterFour

Glenn was absorbed reviewing the final draft of the new report she and Laura had designed when she heard a knock at her door. "Come in," she called automatically, glancing at her watch, surprised that it was already four. She frowned when she saw Liz Edwards.

"Hi," Liz said. "I was wondering if I could talk to you."

Glenn placed the pencil she was holding on her desk. "What is it?"

Liz walked in and sat down. "I have some ideas I want to talk to you about. It's about some of the systems processing."

"What?" Glenn asked incredulously.

Liz held up several pages. "I've been doing some reading and I think I know of a way to get the quarterly closing to execute faster." She hesitated then started to go on.

Glenn cut her off sharply. "You have got to be kidding," she exclaimed, emphasizing each word separately. "You've come in here to tell me how to improve the quarterly closing? I don't believe this."

"No, no," Liz said.

"I think you'd better leave."

"Please," Liz persevered, "can't you give me even five minutes of your time?"

Glenn stared at her, angry, yet thwarted by her obvious determination. "All right," she said. "Five minutes."

Liz rushed into her idea. Glenn listened unwillingly. Though she followed part of what Liz said, she felt her own growing anger prevent her from giving any credence to whatever Liz wanted to explain.

After a few minutes, Liz stopped. She shrugged, held up her pages, and ended, "I've said it all much better in here."

Glenn exhaled in relief. "That's fine. I don't need to read that. Now, your five minutes are up. Goodbye."

"What? Is there something wrong with my idea? What is it?"

"Frankly, I'm not completely clear what your idea is, something about memory expansion or some kind of memory swap, so I gather. It doesn't matter. I'm not interested."

"I don't believe you! How can you dismiss an idea when you don't even know what it is? This is important!"

Glenn saw but ignored the pleading look in Liz's eyes. "Liz, you seem to have forgotten that I'm the one who's in charge here. For the last time, please leave."

"Fine, I'll leave." Liz stood up, obviously angry. She ripped her pages into shreds and flung them into a corner wastebasket as she left the room.

Enraged, Glenn watched Liz leave her office. Oh, she wasn't surprised Liz had wanted to talk to her. Long before now she had wondered when she would ask to do so. But for Liz to come to her with an idea about the quarterly closing—that was too much. Already Glenn had given seven of her working years to Allied Industries, the last three in Materials/Finance. Whatever there was to know about their crippled systems, she knew far better than anyone.

Glenn reached for a straightened paper clip and began jamming it into the partially mangled blotter which covered her desk. Minutes passed while she waited for her anger to ease. Unwanted images of Liz flashed in her mind: seeing her in the cafeteria, in the halls—and at that bar! She had never wanted her around. And now this. Glenn slammed her hand hard against her desk.

"I guess she won't make the mistake of coming in here again!" she exclaimed scornfully, remembering the fear she had seen in Liz's eyes—satisfied Liz wouldn't dare approach her again.

For one moment longer, Glenn felt her outrage hanging suspended. It broke, even as she wished it would not. Another thought forced its way into her consciousness.

"What kind of person am I," she whispered, "that I should take such pleasure in my ability to cause another to feel such fear? When did I become this way?"

Stunned, Glenn stood up and walked over to close her door. She returned and sank into her chair. Suddenly she didn't know what to do.

Liz Edwards—she knew nothing about her. Well, very little, she amended; she had wanted only to forget she had seen Liz at that women's bar. She knew what the others, what Bob and Laura, had said: that Liz was supposed to be very bright. She had never cared to find out. What she knew of Liz was that she came in every day and sat in that office across the hall doing nothing.

"Wrong," Glenn said softly. Liz had been doing something. "And I don't have any idea what that was. Oh, I didn't need this," she moaned. The situation was becoming more complicated by the second. Barely thinking, she picked up her phone.

"Donna, could you ask Liz not to leave? Tell her I'll be over soon. Thanks." Glenn hung up her phone. She didn't know why she had made that call. Something in this was not finished. It couldn't be finished even if Liz packed up and left, which Glenn suspected she was doing right now.

Glenn swiveled in her chair to look through her window. The trees outside the building swayed in the slight breeze. She watched them and tried to think what to do. Certainly she could ignore Liz no longer. At the very least she owed her an apology. Beyond that, she had not a clue what she would do.

It was nearly five o'clock when Glenn walked into Liz's office. "Hi," she said softly, "I didn't know if you'd still be here."

"Oh," Liz glowered, "I suppose you were looking for another reason to fire me?"

"Listen," Glenn tried to interrupt.

"No, I'm finished listening," Liz said, her words exploding violently, her dark eyes burning. "You may think you're some hot-shot manager, but you don't have the slightest idea how to use the people you have. You've done everything possible to force me out of here, so it should gratify you to know you've succeeded!"

"Liz," Glenn said in a surprisingly even tone, "if you're going to insist on berating me, why don't we at least go into

my office? Maybe you'd be willing to continue this in private."
At that she turned and walked back to her own office.

"Now then," Glenn said, closing the door behind Liz,
"what were you saying?"

Liz only stared.

"Okay," Glenn said, "if you're not going to continue,
then let me ask you a question. I'm curious. How did you
learn so much about Materials/Finance operations?"

"I read your damn manuals," Liz said, once again moved
by her anger. "What did you expect me to do, sit here and
rot?"

Glenn closed her eyes. "Liz," she started.

This time it was Liz who cut in. "Okay, I'll tell you what
I think. I think your whole department is screwed up. I didn't
choose to come here, you know. Most of the people in my
program got to pick where they could work this summer. But
no, not me. And you can be damn sure I wouldn't have picked
this company!"

She stopped. Glenn said nothing.

"All I ever wanted to do was work," Liz continued. "How
could that be asking too much? It was supposed to be the
whole idea! I couldn't care less what happened here last year,
and I certainly don't care what you're trying to prove by
ignoring me."

Glenn flushed and looked away. With great effort she
turned back. "Liz," she said, "there's no way I can account for
my actions in these last weeks. I owe you an apology, and
I'm offering that to you. Also, I would like to read the proposal
you've written, but I'm afraid that's impossible now." She
pointed offhandedly to the wastebasket containing the
shredded pages. "Would it be asking too much to get another
copy?"

"I don't believe you!"

"I'm asking that we start over," Glenn insisted calmly.
"I'd rather you not quit. Maybe we can work out a different
ending to this story yet."

Liz looked at her, still disbelieving. Emotion seemed to
drain from her. "I have an extra copy in my office. You can
have it."

She left and returned a moment later.

"Great," Glenn said, smiling warmly as she took the
pages from her hand. "I'll see you tomorrow, then?"

"Yes," Liz said uncertainly. "I'll be here."

"How was the big showdown?" Alice called out cheerfully as Liz approached the sidelines at that night's soccer game.

Liz barely acknowledged her roommate. "Alice, I don't even know where to start," she said as she removed her cleats from her bag and put them on quickly. "I'll tell you the whole story later. If I can remember it."

"Good ending or bad?"

"I don't know. I don't think it has one yet."

Liz took a ball and moved down field to warm up. Still frustrated from her bizarre meeting with Glenn, she kicked the ball hard across the field then jogged after it. It was that last image of Glenn she couldn't shake—when Glenn had reached across the desk to take the pages from her. Liz remembered her inscrutable smile, her blue eyes sparkling entirely too much for someone who had just suffered the full expression of Liz's rage. Glenn had acted as though she didn't care in the least that she had just been yelled at. Liz kicked the ball furiously. Had Glenn been laughing at her?

She looked up when she heard the sharp screech of a whistle. The referee called for team captains in the middle of the field. Liz rejoined her teammates. They were playing in Sudbury tonight; their opponents were young, mostly students home for the summer, many of them members of their collegiate teams. Liz knew she and her teammates were in for stiff competition.

Neither team scored in the first half. On the sidelines during the break Liz picked up a water jug and took a long drink.

"Nice job," Alice said, waiting her turn for the water. "You were running your little legs out there."

Liz handed over the jug and took a deep breath, just now catching her breath. "Thanks. You too."

Alice paused before drinking. An impish grin was on her face. "Is this Glenn's effect on you—turning you into a running machine?"

Liz only shrugged. She wasn't annoyed, but at the moment all she wanted was to ignore the chaotic energy still inside her.

After a brief rest period, the second half started. Just as in the first half, neither team could gain any advantage over the other. Liz ran hard after every ball that came near her. On

51

several occasions she out-muscled her opponent, unseen by the referee, not seeking the physical roughness, but not avoiding it.

Finally she had a chance for a good play. She received a pass from Randi and, out of the corner of her eye, saw Alice sprinting towards the goal. Liz knew that if she could get the ball to her, Alice would score. She tapped the ball several steps in front of her; at that same moment, she sensed two opponents converging on her. Still in the lead by a step, Liz extended her foot. She was just about to clear a pass to Alice when one of the women chasing her tripped her from behind.

Liz cried out as she fell to the ground. Pain, terrible pain, shot through her ankle. Sprawled on the dirt, hands, arms, and knees scraped from the impact, she had no idea why her ankle hurt as it did.

Play stopped. Liz was vaguely aware of the foul called on the woman who had tripped her. Alice and Jeanne were immediately at her side.

"Almost a game-winning play," Alice muttered as she bent over.

Liz sat up and brushed dirt and small stones from her palms. She winced when Jeanne touched her right foot. When she stood, Jeanne and Alice held her, supporting her as she hobbled from the field.

On the sidelines Liz watched in disbelief as her foot continued to swell. For years she had played sports—the past two playing soccer. Not once in all that time had she been hurt.

"How are you doing, Liz?" Jeanne asked after the game ended. They had lost. Their opponents had scored shortly after Liz went out.

Liz shrugged. "Fine. Nice game, Jeanne. You too, Alice." Alice had walked up behind Jeanne.

Jeanne kneeled down. "I hate to say it, but this really does look bad. What do you think about having it x-rayed?"

Liz shook her head. "I'm sure it's not broken. It'll be fine." She started to stand. New pain, sharp and stinging, tore through her. Liz didn't resist when Jeanne and Alice moved closer to steady her.

"Liz—" Jeanne started again when they reached their cars.

"Really Jeanne, it's okay. All I want to do is go home. Alice—"

"At your service," Alice answered in mock formality.

"Call me if you want a ride to the hospital," Jeanne ended. "It doesn't matter what time."

Back in the apartment Liz collapsed on the couch while Alice collected ice and a towel.

"Okay," Alice said after she had wrapped Liz's leg and propped it on two pillows, "the suspense is killing me. What happened at work today?"

"I told Glenn off."

"Oh my god," Alice moaned. "Tell me the whole story."

❋

Glenn spent a quiet evening at home. As a rule she never took work home, but on this night she had made an exception for Liz's proposal.

Glenn's house was located on a small New England lake. Though Glenn knew that some people were born with the need to be near water, she had only acquired her need in recent years. Living in this house had done that to her.

The house had been designed to allow for the greatest possible view of the water. It had two balconies: one was outside of the sliding glass doors in the kitchen; the other was upstairs, just off of the bedroom. Her property extended down a short bank to the water's edge, where a dock gave access to the water.

After unsuccessfully attempting to relax, Glenn took Liz's proposal and went upstairs to the balcony. She settled back into a comfortable chair and in the early evening light proceeded to read the pages.

What Liz had communicated so poorly in her office, hours earlier, Glenn now grasped easily. The concept was simple. It was unbelievable, but if the structure of the computer really was as Liz described it, the proposed procedure should work without difficulty. A few phone calls in the morning and she'd have the answers to her remaining technical questions.

Glenn rested her head on the back of the chair and gazed across the lake. A few small boats weaved in and out of her field of vision. She began to feel more relaxed.

"If I hadn't been able to keep this house," she said softly, thinking this not for the first time, "I don't know what would have become of me." Sighing, she looked back at the pages and wondered about this woman named Liz Edwards. Everyone had tried to tell her that Liz's talents were exceptional. False pride and stubbornness had nearly caused her to make a great mistake.

Glenn was struck by the realization that Liz might still resign the internship. She remembered how angry Liz had been that afternoon; she remembered everything she had said. Glenn smiled. She couldn't recall when someone had last stood up to her. "I deserved it—every last word," she admitted.

Glenn continued to watch the boats on the water. It was as though something had snapped in her today, she thought, trying with little success to put into words her current odd feelings. It seemed to her now that in the last few months she had been on an extended hiatus from the responsibilities in her life. Thinking she was about to leave her job, her home, her life in this city, she had not cared at all for anything soon to be left behind.

The luxury of not caring had exacted a strange toll. Glenn suspected she had hurt people by her attitude. Almost certainly, she had hurt Liz; perhaps there were others. Maybe she had even hurt her close friends. Glenn grimaced, saddened at the thought.

Defensive and callous had never described her before, but on this night Glenn knew she had recently been both. What had happened to her? Had her decision to move altered every aspect of her personality? Or was it only that selfish choices, which one sometimes had to make, could not be made without hurting other people?

"Never mind," she whispered. The questions were too hard.

The light was fading from the western sky, all boats had disappeared from the lake. Glenn smiled as she thought again of Liz—an attractive young woman with a will as strong as her own. Working with her could prove to be interesting.

❁

Had it been any other morning Liz would not have gone to work. Her ankle, swollen twice its normal size, had been painful all through the night. Alice had argued against her going to work. Alice thought she ought to go to an emergency room and have her leg examined, and obviously her head as well. Liz ignored her and left the house, limping severely.

In her office Liz sat at her desk and rested her leg on an adjacent chair. She listened to the activity in the halls as the other members of the department arrived. The sounds by now were familiar; but this morning she listened with a new anxiousness.

Yesterday's events still mystified her. Liz could not begin to explain the transformation in Glenn's attitude towards her—her sudden willingness to consider her idea. She waited, half-believing Glenn's openness to her would turn out to be a momentary aberration. If so, she intended to resign. She could deal with the consequences; what she could no longer deal with was being ignored. The only reason she had come to work today was to find out what would happen.

No, Liz admitted silently, the real reason she was here was because she had promised Glenn she would be.

"I don't know what you succeeded in doing—"

Liz looked up in surprise, unaware Laura had entered her office.

"What happened to you?" Laura said.

Liz grinned to see Laura staring at her misshapen lower leg. "Oh, I got tripped at soccer last night. I twisted my ankle when I fell."

"I can see how swollen it is from here. Did you at least make the other woman look worse?"

"I was about to."

"Liz," Laura continued, "I received a very strange phone call from Glenn a few minutes ago. She wants you to have an account on the system. Here's your access number. Did something happen yesterday?"

Liz's grin expanded. "Yes, you could say that. Unfortunately, I don't know exactly what. It's a long story."

"Give it to me in twenty-five words or less."

"Okay. I worked out an idea about how to speed up the quarterly closing and took it to Glenn yesterday. She looked at it last night. I don't know what she thinks of it."

"So that's what all your questions were about! Honestly, Liz, I was beginning to think you had your own plans for sabotaging our system. Glenn likes something, that much I know. I have to go and see her in a minute. For now she wants you to review the orientation program we have on the computer."

Laura punched a few keys on Liz's keyboard. For the first time in a month, Liz saw words and numbers on the screen.

"Well, here you go. Enjoy the program. My guess is you know it all already."

"Thanks, Laura," Liz said. "For everything."

Liz heard the door to Glenn's office close when Laura went in. A few minutes later the door reopened. Though she half-expected her, Liz was surprised when Glenn appeared in her office.

"Good morning," Glenn said brightly. "How are you this morning?"

Liz quickly removed her leg from the extra chair, ignoring the still-throbbing ache. "Hi. Fine, thanks. How are you?"

"Just fine. I have some good news. Why don't you come into my office, and I'll tell you about it."

Liz stood up and tried to walk. Her ankle buckled immediately under the slight weight she put on it.

"What happened to you?" Glenn asked.

"Oh, I played soccer last night. I hurt my ankle."

Liz was embarrassed by the severity of her limp as she walked the short distance across the hall to Glenn's office. Inside, she sat down in the nearest chair.

"Did you have it x-rayed?" Glenn asked, following behind, pausing to close the door.

"No. My roommate wanted me to, but I don't think it's broken. I think I twisted it when I fell."

Glenn sat down in the chair next to her. "Here, let me look at it. I worked with a local theater company several years ago. During one show's run our dancers and performers had every conceivable sprain, strain, twist, and break. I got to be pretty good at telling them all apart."

Glenn lifted Liz's ankle to her knee and began touching the swollen area. "This is a bad one," she exclaimed softly. "Have you hurt it before?"

"No," Liz answered through gritted teeth. The pain was awful. She stared while Glenn moved her hand from her ankle to her foot, pressing gingerly. Liz gripped the bottom of her chair with both hands, not sure whether she was shaken more by the pain or by having Glenn touch her. She inhaled quiet, deep breaths, vainly trying to calm herself.

Glenn said, "If I take your shoe off I don't think you'll get it on again all summer. This swelling is very bad."

"Please—don't," Liz pleaded as another wave of pain shot through her.

"It's okay. I'm finished. I think you're right, it's not broken. But if the swelling doesn't go down soon you really ought to have it checked. In the meantime—" Glenn broke off when she looked up. "You're so pale!"

Liz closed her eyes when she sensed Glenn's hand moving towards her. She fought back new swells of dizziness, for one instant afraid she might pass out. Glenn's fingers stayed on her forehead another moment; then Glenn lifted a few strands of her hair and pushed them away.

"You're much too warm, Liz. You shouldn't be here."

Liz pulled herself up straight and returned her leg to the floor. "It's okay. I'm all right."

"Don't be silly. I'll tell you why I asked you in here and then I want you to go home. Don't even think about coming in tomorrow."

Liz listened while Glenn quickly and quietly explained that she had read her proposal and was intrigued by the idea.

"I've already talked to the systems people. They think there's a good chance this can work. I want to try it."

Liz smiled weakly.

"This is a big job," Glenn continued, "one I want to monitor carefully. That's why I'm only having you and Laura involved. You know a lot about our computer, Liz. I'm going to need your help. So, what do you think? Are you up for it?"

Liz said that she was.

Glenn smiled a soft smile and said, "Good. You get to start on Monday. For now you go home. Will you be able to drive?"

"Yes. I'll be fine."

A few minutes later Liz left the department. Outside, the smile she had held in check during her slow limp through the building broke wide on her face; she had to restrain herself from leaping up to touch the branches of a tree she passed beneath.

Glenn had touched her. Glenn had spoken kindly. Liz knew Glenn cared about her—if only in some small way.

Chapter Five

Glenn glanced in annoyance at her phone when it rang. Liz stopped speaking and looked expectantly at her.

"Donna will get it," Glenn said. "I'm sorry. Go on."

Liz went on with her explanation. It was Wednesday, Liz's third day on the project, and already Glenn was impressed by how much she knew about their computer and how easily she was able to answer even complicated technical questions.

When Liz finished, Glenn nodded thoughtfully. "But I was under the impression that it is always faster to read by key than it is to obtain a record by doing a sequential read on the file. Why isn't this true in this instance?"

Again Glenn watched Liz closely. As before, Liz frowned; her brow furrowed while she paused to think. But when she started speaking, her expression was clear and candid, her eyes not darting as they often did. Her self-consciousness—at least for the moment—lapsed. Glenn almost smiled. Secretly she wondered whether it wasn't to see Liz so completely unguarded, rather than to hear the answers she gave, that she asked these technical questions.

Glenn scanned her notes after Liz stopped and made a feeble attempt to recall what she had asked. She found the thread and continued. "If I understand what you're saying, then it sounds as though this process could work equally well on several other of our processes."

"Yes. I believe that's true. Assuming it works on this one."

Glenn did smile now. "So what made you choose the quarterly closing for your design?" she asked, making no effort to hide her smile.

Liz blushed, clearly taken aback. "The quarterly closing is a self-contained process," she replied, stumbling slightly in her rush to answer. "There's a lot involved internally, and the closing updates almost all of the production and history files, but it still seemed like an easier process to test and verify than some of the others."

And your decision had nothing to do with your predecessor's malicious screw-up, Glenn asked silently, thinking she knew the real reason Liz had chosen the quarterly closing.

After Liz left, Glenn finished going over the programs Laura had given her earlier. It was just past five; she wasn't meeting Diana and Joyce until six-thirty. Tonight was the first summer concert at the Esplanade—John Williams and the Boston Pops. Glenn wondered which she was looking forward to more: listening to good music sitting near the river on this warm summer evening or sharing the picnic supper Diana had told her Joyce was making.

Glenn pushed Laura's program listing aside and leaned against her desk. She glanced at her desk calendar and realized just one week had passed since Liz had come to her with her idea. Glenn laughed softly. With one brilliant plan and one scathing outburst, Liz had shattered the boundaries she had so carefully set between them.

It was all for the better, that was without question. Glenn smiled faintly, feeling almost guilty for how much she was enjoying her new relationship with Liz. Liz amused her. But that was an unexpected bonus in this whole unexpected situation. The real bonus was that if by some miracle this farfetched plan actually worked, in less than two months she would be leaving Allied Industries on a spectacular high note—thanks, of all things, to Liz.

———

"Laura," Glenn said late Friday morning, "it's been a long week. Would you like to go to lunch today?"

Glenn checked her urge to smile when she saw the look of shock on Laura's face.

Laura recovered quickly. "Oh, I'm sorry. I'd love to, Glenn, but I'm leaving at noon. I have a doctor's appointment today."

"That's right. You did tell me that. Well, we'll go another time." She felt as disappointed as Laura appeared to be.

Glenn had intended to invite Liz as well. Since Laura couldn't go, she almost abandoned her plan. On an impulse, she stopped at Liz's office to ask her anyway.

"Hi. I was wondering if you're free for lunch today."

"I don't have any plans," Liz replied casually, but not before Glenn saw surprise also flashing in her eyes.

"Well, would you consider having lunch with me, despite my belated invitation?"

"I'd like that. Thanks."

They drove into Lexington. It was a long drive, but Glenn remembered an outdoor cafe where she had eaten lunch once before. She breathed a sigh of relief, finding it still open and as nice as she remembered.

Throughout lunch she and Liz talked about the project. Though committed to doing the project now, Glenn still felt occasional moments of pure panic when she doubted this idea had a prayer of working. Glenn wouldn't admit it to anyone, but she was relying on Liz for help with some of the technical details of the plan.

"Tell me about graduate school," Glenn said when she and Liz were nearly finished eating.

"What do you want to know?"

"I don't know. Tell me what you enjoy about it."

Liz hesitated her usual split second. Seeing her lose herself in a first moment of thought, Glenn wished she hadn't wasted so much of their hour talking about work.

Liz described the courses she had taken in her first year and those she planned to take in the coming year. As she spoke, Glenn felt a twinge of envy for the obvious excitement she felt about her work.

"I've often thought of getting a master's degree in computer science," she said when Liz finished.

"What's stopping you?"

"I don't know. I'm not sure it's the right degree for me. An M.B.A. might be more appropriate. Then again, I sometimes question how much I like being in management anyway."

"You'd rather be doing something else?"

"That's a question I don't know the answer to. I've been doing this for so long I've forgotten what other choices exist. Actually, I do like working in data processing. But with all of the changes in the computer industry year to year, I just sometimes wonder what else is out there."

Glenn held her eyes on Liz after she stopped. At first Liz returned her gaze, but then she looked down.

"Your hair, it's very pretty," Glenn said. "Doesn't it bother you to have it so long when you play sports?"

Liz flushed deeply. "Thank you. No, not really. I tie it back. It doesn't get in the way."

"I'm sorry," Glenn said when she saw Liz so uncomfortable. "I seem to always be embarrassing you. I hope you won't be angry with me." Continuing quickly, she said, "Tell me about your soccer team. Do you play in a women's league, or is it mixed?"

Liz looked up, though a trace of pink still showed on her fair skin. "It's only women. I don't know what would happen to me if I played against men."

"I can't imagine either. Are you out for the season, now that your ankle is hurt?"

"No! I'm going to tape it and try to play next week. If I can."

"Really? Well, don't get hurt too badly. Try to remember that your services are needed elsewhere."

Liz smiled.

Glenn hesitated to ask her next question. The words were out before she could censor them. "The other day, you mentioned your roommate. Do you have other roommates or just one?"

"Just one. Her name is Alice. We're on the same soccer team."

"You must be good friends."

"Well, yes, we are. We try to keep each other sane, I suppose," Liz said.

"Oh." Glenn cast her eyes down at the table top. "I live alone. It must be nice to have someone else around."

"Yes, it is. I know what it's like to live alone, too."

Glenn glanced at her watch; she and Liz had been talking for over an hour. "I guess it's time," she said, frowning as she reached for the check.

Liz opened her wallet.

"No, no, this one's on me," Glenn said.

"Oh, no, that's okay."

"No, really. Let me do something to compensate for my atrocious past behavior."

Liz smiled. "Well, okay. Thanks. But it really isn't necessary."

Glenn smiled and said, "Let's go."

❁

The work for phase one of the project came to an end on a Monday afternoon. Liz, Laura, and Glenn worked late, reviewing what they had completed thus far. Testing was scheduled for Tuesday.

The next morning Glenn discovered there had been a mix-up about computer time. She thought the test would take place on Tuesday during the day; the staff in computer operations assumed it would occur Tuesday evening. The operations director gave Glenn no choice in the matter. He informed her that after-hours was the only time his group would be available to her. Disappointed, she told Laura and Liz.

The afternoon dragged slowly on. At five o'clock Glenn made another call to operations, but this one didn't make her any happier: it would be at least one hour, and probably closer to two, before they were ready to go.

Glenn turned around in her chair, noticing for the first time the beautiful summer afternoon. A slight breeze was blowing, the sun was shining brightly. "Rats," she said softly, suddenly unhappy to be stuck inside the building.

Laura walked in. "Is everything set?" she asked.

"No," Glenn replied, swiveling around to face her. "There's another problem. We won't be able to check our files for several hours."

Laura seemed disturbed. "Do we have to wait here until then?"

"Oh, I don't know. I'm trying to think what to do. Why? Is it a problem for you?"

"Well, yes. I could stay for a little while, but I need to be somewhere later on."

"That's all right. Go ahead and leave. We'll probably have to do most of our work tomorrow morning anyway."

"Are you sure?"

"Yes. There's nothing to do here now."

Laura said goodbye and left. Minutes later Glenn walked over to see Liz. "Hi," she said. "Did Laura tell you about the delay?"

"No. What's up?"

Glenn explained the situation. She ended, unsure whether to ask Liz to stay.

"Are you going to stay until the test runs?" Liz asked.

"Yes."

"I'll stay with you if you'd like. I'm not doing anything tonight."

Glenn smiled gratefully. "I appreciate that. But don't feel you have to."

Liz assured her it was no problem.

After painfully enduring the slow passage of another ten minutes, Glenn had a new idea. Briefly, she debated whether she should act on it since it meant breaking one of her cardinal rules. She decided to forget the rule and again went to see Liz.

"I've got a suggestion," she said, walking in.

"Yes," Liz said, her attention obviously distracted by something she was writing.

Glenn frowned, but continued, "Why don't we leave for a couple of hours. My house isn't far. We could spend the time there. Unless, of course, you're too busy."

Liz stopped and looked up. "Are you kidding? That sounds great."

"Well, let's go then."

Fifteen minutes later Glenn pulled into her driveway. Inside, she watched Liz, waiting for the look of surprise to show on her face. She knew Liz hadn't seen the lake from the front.

"This is beautiful!" Liz exclaimed.

"Thanks," Glenn said. "I'm glad you like it."

Liz walked to the windows on the far wall. "I've never seen a house like this. You can see the water from everywhere!"

Glenn enjoyed watching Liz's reaction. She saw her turn around to look at the inside of the house. Liz looked to her right, to the kitchen and beyond it to the deck, visible through the sliding glass doors. She glanced back at the dining room and living room through which they both had just walked. Then her eyes moved to the stairs which lined the inner wall next to the kitchen.

"You can go out on the deck if you'd like," Glenn said, pointing towards the kitchen. "I'll be right there."

A few minutes later she joined Liz. "Oh, I can't believe this day isn't over yet," she said, sighing tiredly as she sat down.

Liz glanced at her and smiled, but she immediately shifted her gaze back to the water. Glenn wondered if she felt uncomfortable. "Where do you live, Liz?" she asked, hoping to put her at ease.

"In Watertown."

Glenn smiled wistfully. "It's been a long time since I've lived in the city. I went to school at Northeastern. I remember when I swore I'd never want to live anywhere but in Back Bay. Where in Watertown?"

"Near Main Street—not far from the river. Do you know the area?"

"Vaguely. I know where Main Street is. Have you been there long?"

"Only a year. I lived in Cambridge before that."

"Was Alice your roommate then?"

"No." Liz laughed. "I moved in with Alice a year ago when I went back to school."

"Why are you laughing?" Glenn asked, unable to keep from smiling.

"Oh, I don't know. Alice is pretty wild. I'm not. I think I was afraid that when I moved in with her my life was going to rage out of control."

"Did it?"

"Much to Alice's disappointment, no."

Glenn flinched suddenly at the thought that Liz and Alice were lovers. That attractive woman she had seen with Liz at the bar—was that Alice? Glenn stood up abruptly and went into the kitchen. So what if they were lovers, she argued silently. She didn't need to be jealous of every woman who had found a happy relationship. She poured two soft drinks and returned to the deck.

Their conversation drifted from one subject to another. When Liz happened to mention the year in which she graduated from college, Glenn interrupted. "You graduated that long ago? How old are you anyway?"

Liz blushed. "I'm twenty-seven. I suppose you thought I was younger."

"Yes, I did. I thought you were twenty-two or twenty-three. I must think all students are that age."

"How old are you?" Liz returned.

Glenn was instantly uncomfortable. She did not want to answer the question; neither could she justify denying Liz her answer. Reluctantly, she said, "I'm thirty, though I never mind when people think I'm older."

"Why? So your authority goes unquestioned?"

Glenn heard the teasing in Liz's voice, but she frowned and looked away.

"Liz," she said, still staring off into the distance, "for some totally inexplicable reason I don't mind telling you things about myself. You know more about me already than Laura's learned in three years." She paused. "I know people at work talk about me. I understand why they do. I've just always tried very hard not to give them anything to talk about."

Looking back, she said, "I guess I'm asking you not to share the things I tell you with the others even if you don't understand my reasons for wanting it that way."

"Don't worry," Liz said hastily, "I won't say anything. I do understand, and I'm sorry if I've upset you."

"No, you haven't. Not really," Glenn responded in the same quiet voice.

It wasn't anger that was causing her to remain quiet, Glenn reflected while driving back to work. She just felt so tired of having to make the effort to keep intact the walls shielding her personal life. She was tired of having to keep her distance from other people. Not all other people, she amended; just people at work. Liz had made her feel conscious of how great an effort that was.

Back in the department Glenn was relieved to escape these thoughts and turn her attention to something concrete. The computer operations staff had finished their part of the testing. She and Liz could now do theirs.

Glenn walked over to Liz's office and instructed her on what to do. "Then, when you're ready to display the files, let me know. I'll come in and look at them, too."

Minutes later Liz appeared in her doorway. "Everything's set," she said.

"Great. I'll be there in a minute."

Liz stood up when Glenn entered her office, offering her chair.

"No, no, you sit there," Glenn said. "Let's look at those files."

Liz sat down and typed in the remaining commands. Glenn walked over and stood behind her. Within seconds the data in their new files appeared. Glenn moved to half sit against the desk; then she leaned forward, squinting to see the tiny characters on the screen. Not thinking, she placed both of her hands on Liz's shoulders. Liz jumped. Glenn squeezed one shoulder and left both hands where they were. Her attention remained fixed on the screen.

Letters and numbers scrolled across the screen. Glenn stared intently; but at the same time she sensed tenseness in Liz's back. Gently, she began rubbing her.

Suddenly the even flow of data broke off. "What's that?" Glenn demanded, gripping Liz more tightly.

"What?"

"That," Glenn said, removing both hands and pointing.

Liz stopped the screen. Glenn was horrified by what she saw. In places where there should have been good data, only garbage—meaningless, incomprehensible characters appeared.

"Where did that come from?"

"I don't know," Liz answered.

"It didn't work. We can't get our data converted."

"No! I'm sure we can."

"Then how?" Glenn demanded. She waited another moment, but when Liz didn't answer, she stood up and left.

Glenn had no idea how much time had passed when she heard Liz enter her office. Her back was to the door; she stared out at the night, watching gray shadows eclipse the last of the day's light.

"I've got something," Liz said tentatively.

"Oh."

"We need to find out what file lengths were used when the data was written. If they weren't changed, that would explain the garbage on the screen."

Glenn spun her chair slowly. She stared at Liz but didn't reply.

"All you have to do is find out whether anyone in operations made that change," Liz said quietly. "I've written down what the new file lengths should be." She held out a page.

"All right," Glenn said. She took the paper from Liz's hand and decided to try her suggestion, not because she thought it would work, but because she simply had nothing better to offer in its place.

She phoned operations. No, they had not changed any file lengths, she learned. The person she was talking to assured her they would do so and would call after rerunning the process.

"Do you really think that's it?" Glenn asked after she hung up.

"At the very least, it is a problem. There may be others we don't know about yet."

"You're encouraging," Glenn said wryly.

For the next twenty minutes they talked quietly. Both jumped noticeably when the phone rang.

"Let's try it," Glenn said after hanging up.

They walked across the hallway to Liz's office. Liz returned to her chair, Glenn to the desk. This time Glenn remained sitting back and it was Liz who peered intently at the screen. The minutes passed slowly; Glenn thought the flow of data would never cease. Finally the last line reached the screen.

This time there were no problems. Liz sighed deeply. She closed her eyes and leaned back in her chair. Glenn smiled at the unmistakable relief she saw flooding through her. She reached over and touched her shoulder. "Good job," she said.

Liz opened her eyes, smiled, and said, "Thanks."

———

Glenn went home that night, unable to stop thinking about Liz. She felt shocked, remembering how completely paralyzed she had become when confronted with their bad data. The memory of Liz's calmness and clear thinking contrasted sharply with the memory of her own unmistakable panic.

"That, however, is the least of my problems," Glenn said to herself as she sat alone in the darkened house.

What she could not forget, what she found herself thinking back to again and again, was the feeling she had had when Liz had leaned back, exhausted, her check of the data complete. At that moment she had had the strongest feeling of wanting to lean over and kiss her.

Chapter Six

Glenn paced restlessly in the lobby of the restaurant in Chestnut Hill. She didn't have to look at her watch to know it was seven o'clock—the time she and Pamela had agreed to meet here. She stopped to watch the lazy, slow-motion movement of a gold and black striped fish inside the large aquarium, centerpiece of the lobby's decor. After eight years of friendship, Glenn knew Pamela would be late—but only a few minutes late. She wondered why that bothered her tonight.

It probably wasn't Pam's history of arriving late that was upsetting her, Glenn finally forced herself to admit. Rather, she was upset at her own unpardonable reluctance to listen to Pamela talk about the woman she had met on her vacation in Provincetown.

Glenn scowled at the gold and black fish then shifted her attention to a tiny fire red one. For the first time in months Pamela was feeling good about herself. She'd just been promoted to Director of Financial Aid at the university and, no less important to Pam, she finally had her hair cut in a way she liked. Now she was excited about her new lover. Glenn felt disgusted with herself for begrudging her any happiness.

Glenn turned from the aquarium and squinted through the glass door, but Pamela was nowhere in sight.

"I could seat you now if you'd like," the maitre d' offered for the second time.

"No, thank you," Glenn replied. "My friend should be here soon."

The man nodded.

Glenn turned back to stare aimlessly at the blue-tinted water. She thought of Liz. Now you're getting somewhere, she conceded, knowing Liz was much more her problem than Pam.

Things had changed between them this week. It was no use pretending otherwise, though for the better part of the day she had done exactly that. Having tried twice to provoke some response in Liz this afternoon and both times only receiving replies of polite distance, she couldn't deny that something had changed.

Tuesday night, Glenn thought, knowing that's when things had changed, at least for her. She laughed silently, but uncomfortably. It was still something of a shock to realize she felt attracted to Liz.

It was almost funny now though, she mused, remembering Tuesday night. Oh, the night had started innocently enough. For a long time after getting home she had teased herself with thoughts of Liz. She had enjoyed the feeling of shock that had coursed through her each time she saw Liz's image in her mind—her long, dark hair and intelligent brown eyes; her solid athlete's body, thin, but strong; her smile, slow in forming, but growing full, as if once loosed she could not stifle it. Each image had produced a stab of feeling, a surge of simple desire to be near this woman. It wasn't sexual; not yet. With any luck—with any restraint on her part—it wouldn't be.

What had started out as innocent teasing became a cruel torment in the late night and early morning hours. Glenn frowned, remembering how she had tossed and turned, unable to sleep. As the night had grown longer, her frustration had turned to anger—anger not just at her unexpected feelings for Liz and at the impossibility of ever being able to act on them; anger, also, at every other thing that was wrong with her life. Glenn knew she had been in a terrible mood that day and most of the next.

But the shock of discovering she was attracted to Liz had faded since then and now Glenn wanted their former casual relationship. Too clearly, something had changed for Liz as well. Glenn frowned, not knowing what. She wondered whether Liz was upset with her because of the way she reacted when the first data test failed. Thinking back to that, Glenn remembered only her panic, but knowing her own history of behaving badly under stress, she worried more that she had said or done something to upset Liz.

"Glenn—sorry I'm late!"

Glenn turned to see Pamela rushing towards her. She smiled warmly and stepped forward to hug her. "That's all right. I'm glad you're here now.

"I do like your haircut," Glenn said to Pamela once they were seated.

Pamela smiled and said, "Thanks." Self-consciously, she brushed her fingers through her hair. "Your hair has such a nice natural curl. I never could hold any curl in mine, and you know how many times I tried!"

Glenn nodded.

Pamela barely paused. "But the other day I suddenly realized this is exactly how my mother has always worn her hair—blunt cut across the front and at the back. Do you know how many months of therapy it's going to take for me to figure out the significance of that?"

Glenn laughed. "Just because you share physical similarities with your mother doesn't mean you have to share any personality similarities. How is your mother, anyway?"

"She's fine. She's coming here next weekend. You know, I'm convinced she's telepathic. Absolutely every time I meet someone new she plans a trip to Boston!"

"I've always said your mother is a woman of exceptional talent," Glenn teased.

"Maybe," Pamela replied noncommittally. "Anything new with your folks?"

"Not that I know of."

They were interrupted by the arrival of two steaming cups of clam chowder. Glenn lifted several spoonfuls, stirring, trying to cool the soup.

"So tell me, what's new?" Pamela asked. "Have you broken any hearts while I've been away?"

Glenn frowned, more annoyed at her own hesitation to ask Pamela about her new lover than she was upset by Pam's familiar teasing. "No. Lately I haven't even gone out with anyone. I don't know, since I've been back from San Francisco, I haven't felt like it."

"What about Miriam? I thought you were seeing her again."

"I was. I have. But you know Miriam. You know me."

Pamela nodded.

Glenn gazed idly at the table, silent for the moment. She would have liked to mention Liz, but she knew what Pamela would try to make of any admission of strong feeling. Instead she said, "Since I'm planning to move soon anyway, there doesn't seem any point to pursuing new relationships."

"You haven't changed your mind then?"

"No. I'm not quite as anxious to leave now, ironically enough as much because of what's going on at work as anything else. But still, once the job offer is made, I will accept it."

"Oh."

"Pam, please, we've been through this before. Let's not ruin the evening talking about it."

Glenn paused for another moment. "There is one thing that we haven't talked about, though. I'm thinking of giving the house back to Diana."

"I wondered about that. I don't think she'll take it, Glenn."

"Why not? It was her house anyway. She just gave it to me because she felt guilty."

Instantly, Glenn regretted the casualness of her reply. Pamela's soft gray eyes flashed with anger. "You know that's not true," she exclaimed. "She gave it to you so that you wouldn't have to be the one to move out!"

Glenn glared across the table at Pamela, stunned at how quickly the old feelings came back. The pain, the anger, the guilt—emotion swept through her like a sudden gust of wind, arising out of nowhere.

"I know, I know. I'm sorry," she said, glancing down. "Maybe I'm the one who feels guilty now. For leaving."

"You really need to talk to Diana," Pamela said softly. "She's more upset at your plans to move than she'll admit to any of us."

Still Glenn couldn't restrain herself. "So she gets to do what she wants with her life and I can't do what I want with mine?" she demanded. "How fair can that be? Pamela, I don't have to take Diana's feelings into account in this decision!"

"Glenn, that's not it. Obviously you don't have to consider her feelings. I'm just telling you she needs to talk about it. Sometimes I wonder whether she's ever resolved her feelings about you two splitting up."

"I don't know whether I can talk about that any more. Maybe I'm not the one for her to talk to."

Tension lingered in the silence that followed. Glenn hated the unbearable hollowness she felt inside.

"Pam, please, let's not talk about this any more. There's no point in our both getting upset," she said, knowing they both already were.

Pamela only nodded.

"So tell me," Glenn went on, "I want to hear about this new woman in your life—Cynthia? For once," Glenn waited until Pamela looked up, "I get to ask all the questions. So, who is she? How did you meet? How many times have you slept with her?"

Pamela laughed at the way Glenn mimicked her. But she gave in and began telling her story.

❀

Liz was furious with herself. She was furious at everything that had happened when she had been at Glenn's house, nearly a week before.

It was Monday morning. A few minutes ago Glenn had rushed into the department and then rushed out, off apparently to an all-day meeting. Liz heard the activity surrounding her entry and exit. Glenn hadn't spoken to her. Now she was gone.

Liz slouched back in her chair and viewed the barrenness of her small office. Laura always teased her about having no photographs or prints on her desk or walls. Sure, Liz thought, whose picture would I bring in? The one of Alice doing a chin-up, wearing those silly red cowboy boots I gave her last Christmas? Or the one of Jennette and Louise, arm-in-arm, braced against the cold when we went to the coast of Maine? Liz snorted. It would not do for her to reveal what paltry pieces of her life she might show—much as Laura hinted she wanted to know more about her.

Glenn was gone for the day. Liz picked up a pencil and thumped the eraser end aimlessly. All weekend she had held onto the hope that Glenn would act differently today. She had been so distant last week. Ever since Tuesday night. Ever since the night they had tested phase one.

Would the real Glenn Kiley—Liz started.

Suddenly a vivid new image of Glenn flashed in her mind, cutting short her light sarcasm. Liz recalled the moment when Glenn had stepped onto the deck at her house, wearing faded blue jeans and scruffy white tennis shoes. She grinned, remembering how hard it had been to turn her eyes from Glenn, how hard it had been to carry on their conversation. Something seemed to have been stripped from Glenn in those fleeting moments—the harshness of her managerial exterior—and Liz had found the casual woman underneath incredibly more attractive.

Then it all changed. Liz felt her grin fade. Glenn had pulled back. Liz didn't know why, could only guess that Glenn had become upset with her. Because she had teased her about her age? Liz grew tense at the memory.

She glanced at the pages on her desk awaiting her attention. Something hardened inside her. Just do your work, she admonished in a low, silent voice.

The truth was she didn't have a clue as to what had caused Glenn to withdraw. Second-guessing Glenn's reasons, and blaming herself for them, seemed equally pointless. Liz scoffed, knowing she wouldn't stop doing either.

———

Monday night Liz played soccer for the first time since she had been hurt. Before the game her ankle had felt fine, maybe a little tender if she stretched it way back. But she had insisted to Jeanne she was ready to play.

The first time she kicked the ball with any force her ankle jarred in searing pain. Liz managed not to fall or cry out, but when the ball glanced off of her opponent then rolled out of bounds, she called for a substitute. Sitting on the sidelines, watching her teammates fall behind by two goals then rally back to take the lead, Liz ached with a longing to be out on the field with them. Relegated to the role of cheerleader, she cheered, but inwardly, she grew depressed.

By the next morning, she felt no better. She sat in her office for a long time only staring at the walls. Her ankle had not remained swollen, yet she had no hope that it had healed. The swelling had been down for a week before she had attempted playing yesterday.

"Hi stranger. Why are you so happy this morning?"

Liz looked up to see Glenn walk into her office. "Oh hi. Three guesses. If one guess is that I hurt my ankle again, you'd be absolutely right."

"Oh Liz, did you play soccer last night?"

Liz shrugged. "I tried to play without taping my ankle. It was a bad decision."

"In case you don't remember, I happen to know something about bad ankles. If you ever need it taped—"

"Glenn, are you in there?" Donna called from the hall.

Glenn walked over to the cubicle entrance. "Yes. What is it?"

"Bob's on the phone. Do you want to take the call?"

Liz saw Glenn frown. "Yes," she answered, "I'll be right there." To Liz she said, "Cheer up. I'll be back to see you later."

At the end of the day Liz was making a half-hearted attempt to arrange her notes and papers when Glenn reappeared unexpectedly.

"Hi. Are you leaving?" Glenn asked.

Liz nodded.

"If you have a few minutes, I'd like to talk."

Liz saw an odd intensity in Glenn's eyes; she felt uncomfortable under their scrutiny. "I have a minute. What's up?"

Glenn hesitated. "Can we go into my office? Better yet, could we go for a walk? Oh, I guess not. You're not getting around very well."

"Actually, I don't have much time," Liz said, surprising herself by holding her distance. "What did you want to talk about?"

Glenn shifted her stance; her bearing seemed to grow more rigid. Almost awkwardly, she said, "I get the feeling something is bothering you. You don't seem very happy, and I'd like to know what's wrong."

Liz averted her eyes as soon as Glenn started. "Nothing's wrong," she said quickly. "I finished another program today. My work is going well."

"I'm not talking about your work. I'm talking about you."

Liz was silent.

"Are you angry with me, Liz?"

"Of course not! Everything's fine. Really. I'm sorry if I've given you the impression it's not."

Neither spoke.

"I've really got to get going," Liz said, feeling even more uncomfortable than Glenn looked.

"All right," Glenn said softly. "Have a nice evening. I'll see you tomorrow."

Liz limped slowly from the building. At her car she stopped to dig in her pocket for her key. She extracted the ring and unlocked the door. Her hand was on the handle when she sensed someone approaching. Before she could turn around a hand touched hers, enfolding it and preventing her from opening her door.

"It's a good thing you're moving so slowly," Glenn said, "otherwise I'd never have caught up with you."

Liz didn't know how to respond. Her stomach felt tight with nervousness.

"Liz, I have to talk to you. Do you really have to leave right now?"

Liz swallowed back her fear. "I'm having dinner with Alice tonight. I guess I have a few minutes."

"Will Alice mind if you're a little late?"

"She'll probably be a lot late."

Glenn seemed uncertain what to do. Then she said, "Let's get in my car, okay?"

Liz nodded.

"There's a small park not far from here," Glenn said. "Do you mind if I drive there?"

"No, that's fine."

At the park they left the car and began walking towards a nearby vacant bench. Glenn smiled for the first time. "It hurts me just seeing how much it hurts you to walk. I don't know what I'm going to do with you—try and talk you out of playing that crazy sport, I think!"

Liz laughed shortly. "No way. I'll never stop playing soccer."

"Liz, there's something I have to ask you," Glenn started when they were sitting down. "Last Tuesday, while we were testing, did you become angry with me because of how I reacted when the first test failed?"

"No, I never thought about it," Liz answered, surprised to know her concern. "At the time all I was thinking about was how to solve the problem."

"Then what's wrong? Why have you been so quiet since then?"

Liz looked away.

"Something happened, and I would very much like to know what it is."

Liz gazed across the lawn to a play area where three children squealed as they jumped on and off a merry-go-round. She thought it too ironic that Glenn thought she was the one who had changed. It didn't seem fair for Glenn not to take some responsibility for the strain between them. Feeling cornered, she said, "I'm not angry about anything. After last week I decided I need to be more serious about work. That's all."

"Why? You've always been serious about your work. You probably work harder than anyone in the department!"

Liz glanced briefly at Glenn before she said, "Well, I guess I didn't want to hear myself asking you any more questions that you didn't want to answer."

Glenn seemed not to know what she was talking about. Then she said, "Are you referring to what we talked about at my house?"

Liz nodded.

"I told you then I don't mind telling you things about myself. I never cared about that!"

For one instant their eyes met intently. Liz searched Glenn's, seeking the explanation for this extraordinary conversation.

Glenn looked away. "I don't like the feeling of having to deny that I have a personal life," she continued. "Believe it or not, I don't ordinarily keep myself wrapped so tightly. It's just that in a work situation everyone is watched so closely. And if ever anyone discovers any little thing to use against someone else, well, you can bet that he or she ultimately will."

Liz remained quiet.

"What am I going to have to do with you?" Glenn exclaimed. "Shake you? Turn you upside-down?"

"No, nothing so drastic," Liz answered, sparing half a smile.

"Look, whatever is going on here, I would very much like to get it cleared up. What's it going to take to make you feel better?"

"Oh, I don't know," Liz answered slowly. "I'm unhappy about my ankle, and I'm worried about all of the work we have to do. Then when I think about the rest of my life I get really depressed."

Glenn laughed. "Join the club. Liz, 'all-the-work-we-have-to-do' is not your worry, it's mine. I'm sure you can't help but wonder how everything is going to turn out. I know I can't. But even if this idea doesn't work, we won't have lost a thing. Are you listening to me?"

77

Liz nodded that she was.

"Your ankle is going to heal in its own time and in its own way. Until then, as long as you get it taped properly, you should be able to continue playing soccer. So then, what's wrong with the rest of your life?"

Liz smiled at Glenn's methodical manner. "Nothing so easy to identify," she said, refusing to admit the role Glenn herself had in her discontent. "Sometimes I don't know what I'm doing in school. Then when I try to think of what I'd rather be doing, I can't name it either. I feel like I'm just muddling through my life."

Glenn smiled sympathetically. "It's tough to find meaningful pursuits in life. Sometimes when you think you've found one, you lose it anyway."

Liz looked at Glenn, struck by the sad tone of her voice. She wondered whether Glenn's sadness had anything to do with someone named D. Brant—the name she had seen next to Glenn's, either faded or erased, near the doorbell at her house.

"Work has never been a problem for me," Glenn went on. "I've worked at Allied since before I finished college. For me, it's like a game that I like to play well. Sometimes I'm more caught up in it, sometimes less so. As you've probably noticed, I have a tendency to panic when I think I'm not playing it well."

For a while they sat in silence.

"Oh Liz," Glenn said, "life is so complicated. Let's not complicate it more. Just be yourself. I enjoy talking to you. Don't try to change, okay?"

Liz blushed. "No, I won't. Glenn, I do feel better. Thanks."

"Anytime," Glenn said. She reached over and shook Liz playfully. "I guess we'd better go. I don't want Alice to be angry that I've kept you."

———

"Don't tell me, let me guess," Alice said to Liz when they met for dinner that night. "You're either Mopey, Dopey, or the Cat Who Ate the Canary."

"Swallowed," Liz corrected.

"Swallowed what?"

"The Cat Who Swallowed the Canary."

"Is that who you are?"

Liz rolled her eyes, realizing as she did so this was a frequent response of hers to Alice. "No," she said.

"All right, then you tell me."

Liz pushed the food around on her plate then stabbed a piece of chicken with her fork. She and Alice were eating at one of their favorite restaurants, a Greek diner in Watertown.

"There's nothing to tell! Glenn wanted to talk after work; she thought I was mad about something, I don't know what. So we talked. It's no big deal." Even as she said the words, Liz knew she didn't want to believe them.

"Were you?"

"What?"

"Mad about something."

"Well, no. I wasn't feeling so great, but it didn't have anything—"

"Liz, you don't have to tell me how you've been for the last week. I live with you, remember? This woman makes you crazy. Something's going on here, I can't wait to see what. Do you want to go to the bar tonight to see if Glenn shows up?"

"No!" All at once Liz had a vivid image of Alice and her at the bar and Glenn walking in. Alice would probably try flirting with Liz, hoping to make Glenn jealous. Glenn already suspected she and Alice were lovers—at least that's what she thought after hearing Glenn's parting comment tonight.

"Tell me truthfully, Liz, do you think Glenn is interested in you?"

"No! I think she likes me, but she has a hard enough time dealing with that. I think she prefers it when she's barely on speaking terms with her co-workers."

"How lovely."

"What's going on with you these days," Liz asked, anxious to change the subject. "How's Carol?"

"Married."

Alice's voice sounded unusually flat. Liz did not believe she could be serious, but when Alice looked up, Liz knew by the look in her eyes that she was.

"What? When did you find out?"

"Over the weekend. She said she'd call on Monday. Silly me, I wanted to see her on Saturday even though she said she'd be busy. Busy! I'll say."

"What happened? Did you go to her house?"

"No. I called. This man answered the phone and when I asked to speak to Carol he bellowed out 'It's for you, dear.' I hung up." Alice was quiet. "I did talk to her on Monday. She called, apologized, said she knew it had been me." The next time Alice looked up more life showed in her eyes. "Her husband works in Chicago and commutes home every other weekend. Carol wanted to know if this would make a difference to our relationship. I asked her what relationship. Ha!"

Liz wished she knew some magic that would ease the unexpected sadness she saw in Alice.

"I guess we'd better keep that reservation we have at the Lesbians Old Age Home," she said quietly, a smile on her face and in her eyes. "It looks like we'll be driving each other crazy until the next millenium."

"It isn't as bad a life as all that, is it?"

"Not bad at all. Oh, let's go to the bar. I'll beat you at a game of pool."

"Try it," Alice said, challenge rising in her voice, "You've never beaten me yet." More softly, she said, "You may be nuts, Edwards, but you're a nice kind of nuts."

❧

"Glenn, can I talk to you a minute?"

Glenn glanced at Bob and nodded. She had just pushed her chair back from the table and was anxious to leave, bored witless by the two-hour managers' meeting that had just ended.

After the others left the conference room, Bob closed the door and sat down next to her. "A question for you," he said. "What exactly is going on in your department these days? Helen showed me time sheets from your group. If I remember correctly, more than ninety percent of Laura's time and over fifty percent of your time in the last weeks have been spent on some special project. Would you mind telling me what that is?"

Glenn tensed. "It's a special project," she said, a noticeable edge in her voice. "We're working on an alternative method for running the quarterly closing. I believe this approach will enable the closing to run considerably faster than it does at present."

Bob nodded slowly. "Two questions, then. First, where did you get this idea, and second, why didn't you request permission before undertaking such a project?"

Glenn turned away, sensing she had flushed. "The answer to your first question is that Liz Edwards developed the idea. The answer to your second is, in your own words, I believe, you said I had to decide what's best for my department. Why? Is there some problem?"

"The problem, Glenn, is that you and Laura represent the major resources in your department. You can't afford—oh, never mind." Bob stopped and stared at her. "How much longer do you think it will take to test this little theory of yours?"

Glenn braced herself. "I'm not sure. It could take another three weeks."

"Three weeks! My god, Glenn, have you lost your mind?"

Glenn returned his angry stare. No, but if I work here long enough I will, she thought but did not say.

A short, ugly silence followed. Glenn realized, belatedly, that Bob had the authority to cancel the entire project. Not for anything did she want that to happen.

"Bob, I'm sorry I didn't mention this to you. I don't know what I was thinking. Originally I didn't anticipate it taking this long. In my office I have detailed plans describing what we're doing. Could you at least look at them before you decide I can't continue with this?"

Bob grudgingly consented. As Glenn was about to leave, he said, "I think you've shown lousy judgment on this one, Glenn. Liz Edwards was supposed to help you with your existing work, not reconfigure the architecture of your systems. I won't allow this 'special project' of yours to be an excuse for not getting any of your other work in on time. Do you understand me?"

"Yes. I understand perfectly," Glenn replied, struggling to contain her indignation.

Ten minutes after Glenn returned to her office, Liz knocked at her door and asked to come in.

"I think I got confused about what my program should be doing," Liz said, holding out a page that described her current task.

Glenn took the paper and scanned it. "Right, both functions should write to temporary files," she said. "The program Laura is working on will use that to update the master files."

Liz frowned and looked unhappy.

"What's wrong?" Glenn asked.

"I thought my program was supposed to change the master files. I screwed up."

Glenn held up the page Liz had given her. "But Liz, it says right here which files to write to."

"I know, I know. I'm sorry. I don't know how I missed it."

"How far did you get?"

"I was working on 121 through 125. I'll have to go back and change all five now."

Glenn felt new frustration. She did not need for Liz—or Laura—to be making foolish mistakes, especially not now. "Liz, ask next time if you're not sure, okay?" she said, trying to keep disappointment out of her voice.

Liz nodded and left the room.

The day went from bad to worse, then from worse to disastrous. Glenn worked behind her closed door battling one problem after another. The final straw came late in the afternoon when she discovered that Kathy Green did not have the reports finished that were her responsibility to produce. After a loud and angry confrontation in the hall, Glenn told Kathy she'd run the reports herself. Now it was past seven o'clock. But everything was finished.

Stepping out of her office, Glenn saw the faint glow of a florescent light coming from Liz's cubicle.

"What are you doing here?" she asked, entering unannounced and finding Liz at her desk.

"Fixing my programs. I'm nearly done." Liz stretched her arms behind her head and yawned.

Glenn walked in and leaned against the wall. "You didn't have to stay late to do that. You work fast enough anyway."

"Yeah, well, maybe too fast. It doesn't matter. It's done."

Glenn rested her head against the fabric of the cubicle and looked up at the ceiling. She rocked lightly, one foot bent touching the wall. "I want a drink," she said decisively. "Do you want a drink?"

Liz smiled. "I would love a drink."

They drove to a restaurant on the edge of town and were seated in a large corner booth.

"I did not have a good day," Glenn said. "I guess you didn't, either."

"I don't think it was as bad as yours."

"Oh, that Kathy makes me so mad," Glenn exclaimed. Liz nodded when she asked if she had heard their exchange in the hall. "Her work can be so good. Usually it is. Then every once in a while she pulls a trick like today. She just waited too long to run those reports."

"So what'll happen now?"

"It's done. I ran them myself tonight. I bumped the priority on my account so they'd run more quickly. I hate monopolizing the system like that, but at least we'll have reports for the managers tomorrow."

"So that's why the system was so slow!"

Glenn felt embarrassment creep into her face. "Sorry. I really didn't have much choice."

Glenn took a first sip of her drink. "I hate it when I get so upset. Every time it happens I tell myself I won't let it happen again, that I'm not going to overreact. Then I do anyway."

"Why do you think it happens?"

Glenn felt her facial muscles tighten. "Frustration. Not wanting to be taken advantage of. I guess lately I've been more than a little frustrated with my life."

Glenn regretted allowing their conversation to move so closely into her life. "You didn't have any plans tonight?" she asked, anxious to change the subject.

"No. Last night was soccer night."

Glenn sipped from her wine glass. "I'll be glad when we finish phase two of the project. This is the most time-consuming part. Even so, I think you and Laura will finish next week."

Liz nodded.

"If all of this works, then the next time we have to run system reports it won't take three days!"

Again Liz agreed.

"Sorry. I don't mean to take my frustration out on you, of all people." Glenn stopped. "Just for the record," she continued more quietly, "I don't talk like this with anyone else from work. For some reason I feel comfortable talking to you, Liz. I don't know, I guess it's because you know about my sexuality."

"That night in the bar. I didn't know if you recognized me."

"Oh yes. I didn't want to admit it. As you know, I try to keep my sexuality—and most of my personal life—separate from my life at work. Was that Alice you were with?"

"No. It was Jeanne, a friend from soccer."

Glenn nodded. In a stronger tone she said, "I'm glad it hasn't been a big deal. I appreciate your discretion." She paused just barely. "So, are you involved with Alice?" As soon as the words were out she rushed to add, "You don't have to answer. I don't want to pry."

Liz laughed nervously. "It's okay. No, I'm not involved with Alice. I'm not involved with anyone right now."

"Me neither."

Glenn was grateful for the dim lighting which hid the color in her face. Not that Liz would have noticed—her eyes were lowered. Glenn felt a slow warmth moving through her. She knew that her flushed feeling was more than discomfort at their mutual admissions. She liked being this close to Liz. She wished she dared risk moving closer.

But that was the one thing she could not do. Her reasons hadn't changed—she and Liz had to work together; she was still moving to California.

"As long as this is already an outrageous conversation," Glenn continued, "I have a confession to make. A week or so ago I went to watch one of your soccer games. I heard you tell Laura where you were playing. It was near here."

"I didn't see you!"

"No, I stayed in the distance. But I did see you. And I have to tell you something—I hope you won't be offended."

Liz shook her head.

"I was impressed. You're a very good player, but that's not what I'm talking about. You love that game. That was so clear to me. Now I understand why you were so upset when you couldn't play."

"I do like to play," Liz affirmed.

"What do you like so much about it?"

Liz glanced at her, then gazed past her. Glenn saw that lost look again in her eyes—as if Liz was lost somewhere deep inside herself—and she felt a stronger stab of desire to know that place in her.

Liz spoke softly. "I guess I like losing myself for ninety minutes while the game is being played. I like trying to get the ball away from someone or shooting at the goal myself. It's a thrill, an unbelievable thrill to do something right, really right, something that shows and something everyone on the team appreciates." Passion spilled into her voice. "I guess that sounds silly," she ended.

"Not at all. I'm jealous of what you have."

Liz scoffed. "Of what?"

"Feeling. You have strong feeling. I don't have that."

Tentativeness disappeared from Liz's expression. "Why did you want to watch a silly soccer game?" she asked, almost demanding, defensive in her embarrassment.

Glenn, too, became defensive. Her hands moved nervously on her wine glass and her voice faltered. "I have a lot of time on my hands right now. There are some things in my life which I don't feel awfully happy about. Let's just say that I found watching you play soccer good entertainment for a summer evening."

There was a moment of silence.

"Tomorrow's my birthday," Glenn said, hardly knowing what she was saying. "I'll be thirty-one. Do you want to know something? I feel like I don't have a single important thing to show for my life."

Liz stared helplessly. "Happy birthday tomorrow," she said.

Chapter Seven

The heat of summer had settled over Boston and its suburbs; hot, humid days followed hot, humid nights, the cycle repeating itself for days on end. Only the early mornings retained any of the nights' slight coolness. It was late July. Knowing that August was, historically, both hotter and more humid, already Liz dreaded the approach of the coming month.

Occasionally in the mornings she coaxed herself into rising early and going for a run. She was always well-rewarded for her effort. The world was nearly still at 6 a.m. Blue sky with white-flecked clouds set the backdrop for the new show of the sun's golden light. The grass was wet and the air felt fresh; by eight o'clock neither would be true.

One morning Liz went for a half-hour run and returned to the apartment for breakfast. She filled the coffee pot only half full with water. Alice hadn't been home last night; Liz frowned, remembering Alice hadn't been around much lately. Not since she had stopped seeing Carol. She spent her nights at the bars, then in the beds of old lovers or new ones. Liz couldn't keep track. Some days she was angry that Alice was gone so much. It was hard to keep coming home to an empty house—more than that, she missed having Alice to talk to. Then, imagining Alice's responses to her so-called problems, Liz wondered whether it wasn't best that Alice never had the chance to make those replies.

What would this day bring, she wondered. She never knew what to expect from any day. Some days, after morning meetings, she, Glenn, and Laura would go to lunch. Some days, Glenn would appear in her office late in the afternoon for no apparent reason other than to talk. One night Glenn had even invited her and Laura out for a drink after work. But there were other days, days when Glenn was aloof and distant, as cool as she had been when Liz first knew her.

The schedule for the project had slipped by two weeks. Liz knew they would be lucky now to finish by the time her internship ended. She and Laura often worked late trying to meet their deadlines. And Laura was frequently pulled off for other projects. It was an aggressive schedule; no one denied that. Yet neither she nor Laura wanted that to become an excuse for their failure to complete it on time.

Liz looked up and saw that the coffee was ready. She went into the kitchen and pushed the start button on the toaster. Would anything happen today, she wondered again; would anything happen that would tell her, one way or the other, whether Glenn was interested in her? It was the only question she cared about, the one almost always on her mind. Since that night she and Glenn had gone out after work alone, she had wondered about this. Glenn never said anything that revealed her feelings. But sometimes, when Glenn looked at her, Liz saw her expression, her whole face, seemingly soften with warmth, that look betraying the feelings she wanted to believe existed.

If Alice was home, Liz thought, imagining their conversation, Alice would say, "Go for it, Edwards—let her know you're interested." Liz was certain Alice would not condone her wait-and-see attitude. But Alice didn't know Glenn. Alice didn't know how rarely Glenn relaxed from her defensive posture nor how quickly she was prone to revert to it.

Liz swallowed the last of her first cup of coffee. She stood to go and dress for work. Maybe another day she would approach Glenn differently. Sure, she thought sarcastically, knowing she wouldn't. She would leave it to Glenn to make the first move—assuming first, or any, moves would ever be made.

Monday afternoon Liz worked until six then rushed to the soccer game, certain she would be late. The field wasn't far from her building; still, she was surprised to find she was the first of her team to arrive. She lay down in the cool grass and waited for her friends.

Several players from the opposing team were putting up goal nets. Liz heard the sound of their voices, their words indistinguishable. She rolled on her back and looked up at the cloud-draped sky. Rain was forecast, but so far none had fallen.

Liz closed her eyes and took deep breaths to relax. It had been a good day, a very good, very normal day. She had made steady progress on her work. And both Glenn and Laura had been in great moods. Liz smiled, recalling the way they had teased each other at this morning's meeting.

"Well, if it isn't the long-lost workaholic!"

Liz turned when she heard Alice's voice.

"I didn't know if you would spare time for our game," Alice said.

"I've never missed a game yet, except for when I couldn't play anyway," Liz returned.

"Has Glenn set up a cot for you in your office?" Alice continued. "That way you'd never have to bother coming home, and who knows what might happen between you two then?"

Liz threw a soccer ball hard at Alice. "What is your problem?" she demanded.

Alice shrugged. She dropped her long, lean frame down next to Liz. "I don't know. Don't tell anyone," she said, lowering her voice to a whisper, "but I miss your gloomy presence in the apartment."

Liz did not deign to reply. She stood up, took the ball she had just thrown at Alice, and moved further down the field. "You're a fine one to talk," she shouted back. "You haven't been around much either!"

After the game, which their team won easily, Liz stopped with the team to get something to eat. Alice slid along the bench to sit next to her.

"Nice game," Liz said. Alice had scored the first and last of their goals.

"Thanks. You too. Want to split an order of something?" she asked, already scanning the menu.

"Sure."

Glasses of water were passed around the table. Liz listened while Mary, sitting across from her, complained loudly and angrily to Jeanne about some call late in the game.

So what, she thought. The game was over. She took a long drink and wondered what this group would get into tonight. Jeanne always came up with something outrageous for them to talk about. After the other night's game they had had a heated discussion over the question of whether scientists can be any more objective in their quest for truth than so-called experts in other, less quantifiable fields. Liz couldn't imagine where Jeanne found the ideas she suggested they talk about. "She reads the *New Yorker,*" Alice had answered when Liz asked her about this once.

"Can I ride home with you?" Alice asked Liz an hour later as the group began breaking up.

"Sure. If you promise to be nice," Liz added even though ninety minutes of soccer seemed to have taken the edge off of Alice's caustic humor.

"Ah Liz, you know that's a promise I can't keep."

At the car Alice leaned against the roof and waited for Liz to unlock the passenger door. "Oh Liz, this summer's not turning out to be what either of us expected, is it?"

Liz looked over and saw Alice's sweat-dampened dark curls and bright brown eyes. She felt a surge of affection for her attractive, talented roommate even as she thought that Alice could sometimes be one of the most infuriating people she knew.

"The summer's not over, Alice."

Alice mumbled something as she got into the car; Liz only caught the part about madwomen and decided not to pursue it.

———

On Wednesday afternoon the storm broke. A huge thunderstorm rolled through the area dropping buckets of water on the dry land. It was almost a relief, Liz thought, watching it from a hall window. The clouds had been thickening since Monday.

At five-thirty she went into Glenn's office and handed in her latest completed task.

"No soccer tonight? Isn't this a game night?" Glenn asked.

"Have you looked out your window recently?" Liz said by way of reply, elated that Glenn knew her schedule so well. She slouched down in a chair.

Glenn leaned on her desk, her chin cupped in her hands. "Oh, I forgot. It is awfully messy out there. You look beat."

"I feel it."

"Listen, if you're not doing anything tonight, why don't I cook you dinner? It's the least I can do to thank you for all of your work."

"You don't have to thank me," Liz blurted too quickly. "Really, I'm enjoying this." Then she looked at Glenn, suddenly unsure what she had said.

Glenn's expression showed pure exasperation. "Well, if you're going to insist on being difficult, what if I said I just wanted to have dinner with you?"

"Dinner sounds great," Liz said, laughing at the thought that she must be more tired than she realized to have come that close to forfeiting Glenn's invitation.

Liz drove her own car to Glenn's house. For the second time she followed Glenn up the front steps and entered the house she had thought of so often. Glenn took in her mail and went upstairs to change clothes.

Liz sat down in the living room. On the coffee table in front of her she noticed several magazines; leaning forward, she saw the latest issues of *Ms.*, *Time*, and *Businessweek*. Only the last surprised her. Either Glenn was serious enough about her career to want to keep up with current trends—or, Liz thought, she must be genuinely interested in business.

The glass-topped coffee table itself was beautiful. Liz touched the blonde wood into which the glass was inset. Curious now, she noticed the other furniture in the room: the large, soft, chocolate-brown sofa on which she was sitting; a matching love seat adjacent at one corner; another chair at the other end. Across from her an entertainment center held a TV, VCR, and stereo. Nice things—expensive, Liz thought, thinking her and Alice's secondhand furniture seemed shabby by comparison.

Liz rested her head against the back of the couch and closed her eyes. Abruptly, she sat up, thinking she heard Glenn coming downstairs. When Glenn didn't appear she relaxed and returned to her momentarily suspended thought.

She had, of course, been thinking about Glenn. Nothing new about that. Liz wondered what would happen between them tonight and felt slightly panicked. Tired from the long days of working, she hoped Glenn would not try to engage her in one of their frequent, mock arguments. Tonight she did not feel interested in verbal sparring.

Glenn still had not appeared. To amuse herself, Liz went to the bookcase behind the couch. She was surprised at the range of titles she found on the shelves: novels by D.H. Lawrence, Thomas Hardy, Jane Austen, and the Brontë sisters; Emily Dickinson's poetry; a huge hardcover edition of the complete works of Shakespeare.

Liz stopped at a book that seemed out of place. She picked it up, grinning as she read the full title—*The Tao of Wall Street: Investment Strategies for the World-Weary*. She opened the front cover, instantly freezing when she saw the initials D.B. inked in one corner. Hurriedly, she replaced the book on the shelf.

"Looking for something to read?" Glenn said.

Liz turned when she heard Glenn on the stairs. "Not tonight, thanks. Have you read all of these books?" she asked.

Glenn nodded.

"What did you study in college?" Liz asked as she returned to the couch.

"English literature. Why do you look so surprised?"

"I don't know. I would have guessed it was business administration or information processing, I think."

Glenn sat down in the chair. "Because I'm so good at what I do?"

"Well, yes."

"Believe me, the amount of talent it takes to be successful in business you can find inside of a comic book."

"I don't believe you. I think you're a good manager, and I think you work hard at it."

"Maybe I do," Glenn admitted. "Can I get you a glass of wine? I'm going to have one."

"I'd love one."

Glenn returned from the kitchen with two glasses. Twenty minutes passed before Glenn said, "Well, if we're going to have anything to eat tonight, I'd better get started."

Liz followed her into the kitchen. Before she knew it, they were both sitting at the table slicing the freshly washed vegetables.

Rain had started falling again. Liz turned from the table to look through the windows behind her. Raindrops seemed to be ripping at the surface of the lake, cutting holes, each drop creating its own new splash. Distant thunder sounded across the lake. Liz smiled and turned back to see Glenn also watching the storm.

Her eyes scanned Glenn's tired, somber face. This wasn't the Glenn she knew, Liz thought, the awareness flashing through her just as the streaks of lightning flashed in the dark sky. The Glenn she knew was the one who donned the mask of a business suit, whom she saw day after day in the sterile offices of Allied Industries. But this was the Glenn she wanted to know.

Glenn's focus fell back to the kitchen. "I didn't promise you anything fancy," she said, breaking their brief silence. She pulled out a casserole dish and arranged the vegetables in it.

Glenn finished preparing their dinner. She opened the oven and placed the dish on the shelf. After setting the timer she returned to her seat. While they were talking, Liz noticed Glenn rotating her head from side to side, apparently stretching her neck muscles.

"So you're tired too?" she said.

"Yes, I am. You don't have a monopoly on that tonight." Glenn finished her wine.

"Can I get you more?" Liz offered.

"Well, yes, thanks. I don't have to drive anywhere tonight."

Liz refilled Glenn's glass. Then, instead of returning to her own chair, on an impulse she went to where Glenn was sitting. Standing behind her, she began rubbing her shoulders.

"Oh Liz, that feels wonderful."

Liz pressed her fingers into Glenn's back and into the thin, tense muscles of her shoulders. A smile of disbelief settled on her face. She could not believe her own nerve in initiating this contact.

"I think I might never let you stop this," Glenn said dreamily after several minutes had passed.

"Don't worry, I don't have any urgent appointments."

Glenn smiled and closed her eyes.

Liz worked her hands back and forth across Glenn's shoulders. She stared at the line Glenn's hair drew across her shirt collar and wished she had the nerve to reach to the skin beneath, to stroke her scalp, and to caress her neck. Instead she kept her hands safely within the bounds set by Glenn's shirt.

After a while Liz thought she could sense Glenn's muscles loosening. Glenn sat up straighter and moved her shoulders back and forth. "Much better," she said. "Thank you."

Glenn stood up to check the oven timer. "Will you allow me to return the favor?" she asked. Liz nodded in a way she hoped was noncommittal. "Oh, this is nearly done," Glenn said after glancing at the clock.

Liz stood up and retrieved two plates from a cabinet. Glenn spooned rice onto a serving dish and placed it and the casserole on the table. She and Liz sat down to eat.

"Tell me," Glenn said, "where did you learn to give such good back rubs? You zeroed in on all of my tight muscles."

"Oh." Liz laughed uncomfortably. "From Alice. She works part-time at a health club during the winter, and she's learned a lot there. Her regular job is repairing stereo and electronics equipment, but she works at the health club so she can use their weight machines."

"Does Alice have a nice body?"

"Really nice. Alice has muscles in places I didn't know muscles existed." Liz spoke enthusiastically then broke off in deep embarrassment.

Glenn laughed. "I'd like to meet her sometime."

After that they were both quiet. Liz was surprised to feel suddenly nervous. The mood between them seemed so intimate, but she didn't know what the occasion was: whether it was an unremarkable dinner or a precursor to something else. And if the night was leading somewhere else, Liz wondered when or how she'd know that.

"I hate to say it," Glenn said after they had finished eating and had cleared the table, "but all I feel up for is watching TV. What about you?"

"TV's fine with me," Liz replied.

Glenn found a movie that was about to start. At best, it sounded mildly entertaining; for the moment it served their purpose. They sat down on the couch to watch it.

When the phone rang an hour later, Liz jumped in surprise.

"Expecting any calls?" Glenn asked as she slid towards the far end of the couch to answer it.

Liz just smiled.

"Hello," Glenn said.

Liz continued to watch the movie, but she couldn't help overhearing Glenn's side of the conversation. Glenn's replies were short, as if she were being careful to say little. When she exclaimed, "Diana!" Liz tensed, taken aback.

"Soon. I'll call you soon," Glenn said, then, "Yes. Good-night, Diana."

Glenn hung up. "Sorry," she said, sliding back, this time moving closer.

They both returned to watching the movie. Liz tried to pay attention to the story, but her mind kept drifting away—to Diana, whoever Diana was.

Forget it, she warned, feeling herself becoming upset. But she couldn't forget—not the phone call, not the warmth she had heard in Glenn's voice. Liz realized she resented the caller. She resented her intrusion.

Into what, she asked herself sarcastically.

Into nothing. Probably nothing.

Just an ordinary night, a dinner with my boss, she insisted in pained silence. Liz tensed against a surge of new jealousy. Diana almost certainly was somewhere on the inside of Glenn's life. And she remained on the outside.

As the minutes passed, Liz began to feel terrified. She could not go on pretending everything was all right. It wasn't. She wanted more, much more from Glenn. But she knew she would never let herself say this.

Finally the movie ended. "Not the greatest drama I've ever seen," Glenn said as she stood to turn the TV off. "But the company was nice."

Liz remained quiet.

"Why are you being so noisy?" Glenn teased as she returned to the couch.

Liz was in no mood for teasing. She only shrugged.

"Hey, what is it?"

Liz felt Glenn sit down and move close. Then Glenn reached over and put one arm around her. Liz could not bear this. She didn't know what was happening. Then she felt Glenn touching her with her other hand, gently moving her fingers through her hair. As Glenn pushed the long strands away from her face, Liz knew her confusion was about to be visible.

"What is it, Liz?"

Liz raised her head slowly. "I like you, Glenn. I like you very much," she said, not knowing anything else to say. Immediately, she looked down.

"I like you, too," Glenn said.

Glenn nudged her head and Liz looked up again. Glenn's eyes sparkled. She did not seem the least bit uncomfortable with their closeness. Liz felt Glenn's arm still around her; she saw her other hand, lying between them. Hesitantly, she reached to touch it.

"Well, it's late," Glenn said, moving away. "Maybe we'd better call it a night."

Glenn's words were the last thing Liz expected to hear. Too clearly, Glenn meant for her to leave. Feeling upset, and embarrassed, and filled with emotions she could no longer control, Liz stood and rushed for the door. Glenn followed her. Just before she was at the door, Liz felt Glenn touch her shoulder.

"Liz."

Liz half turned.

Glenn stepped forward. She put her arms out and Liz felt herself drawn into them. Glenn held her close.

"I'm sorry," Liz said, "I'm just really tired."

"It's all right." Glenn stepped back. "I'll see you tomorrow, okay?"

Liz nodded. She turned and walked rapidly down the steps.

Liz carefully backed her car out of Glenn's driveway then turned onto the street. Moving forward, she pressed the accelerator to the floor and gripped the steering wheel with her hands. Her eyes focused rigidly on the road. Mechanically, she guided the now speeding car around each new curve and bend.

Her mind was filled with a screaming tirade, words and thoughts indistinguishable. To drown it, Liz turned on the radio, pushing the volume to its loudest setting. Willing herself to feel nothing, to think nothing, she drove through the mostly empty streets. Somehow she managed to get home without incident.

The memory of Glenn's phone call stayed in her mind. Liz could guess, only too well, what the other had said simply from having heard Glenn's responses. Diana! Could this be the D. Brant, clearly written on Glenn's door? Liz argued over and over with herself, the stronger, more rational argument saying no, of course not, there are so many names that begin with D. In her current mood Liz was inclined to believe the other argument, the one that said of course there is a Diana Brant, who is in fact Glenn's lover, and who commutes in on weekends from Chicago!

Liz buried her head in her pillow and tried to quiet these raging thoughts. She didn't succeed. Nor could she succeed in denying any longer the painful awareness that she had fallen in love with Glenn.

❁

The next morning promised to be a disaster. Liz went to work early after a brief debate in which she considered not going in at all. The prospect of spending the day alone held no appeal either.

As soon as she heard Glenn's voice in the hallway, Liz knew she could not risk an encounter. If Glenn asked even one of her typical, probing questions, Liz knew she would fall apart. She slipped out of her office and went to the cafeteria.

Much later, she returned. The department seemed unusually quiet. Liz wondered why Glenn never came in to see her. She wondered whether Glenn was angry with her. But for what—for having misinterpreted something last night? Liz shuddered, still confused at how the night had ended. Then cool anger replaced her unsettled emotions and she wondered why it was all right for Glenn to move as close to her as she liked—then pull back without warning or explanation.

The morning wore on. Eventually, Liz gave up all pretense of working and only stared dazedly at the walls. Sometime later Laura came in.

"What truck hit you?" Laura asked.

Liz snapped to attention. "I think it's called phase two," she answered, hoping her voice sounded normal.

"Well then, thank god it's almost over. I think I feel almost as bad as you look."

Laura told Liz that she and Glenn had attended a meeting that morning; she said Glenn had gone out to lunch.

"I think I'm going to leave early," Liz said. "I have to go to school and pay my registration fee. Do you think Glenn will mind?"

"Are you kidding? Not after all of the work you've been doing here. I know she was looking for you earlier, but I'll tell her you left. Go pay your bill, then go home and get some sleep."

Liz smiled quickly—at Laura's kindness, but more to hide her newly jarred emotions. "Thanks. I think I will. But what about you? You've been working just as hard as I have."

"Oh, I'm okay. Besides, I get paid decently for this. As many hours as you've been working, I'll bet you're not even making minimum wage any more."

Soon afterwards, Liz left. She ignored Laura's suggestion about going home to catch up on her sleep. Instead, she filled her car with gas and drove west to I-495. Then, heading north, she drove the familiar road that would take her to Maine.

———

Liz didn't turn around when she heard Alice enter the apartment. Wade Boggs was at bat. The tying run was at third.

"I said hello," Alice called out over the whirring of the small fan which only seemed to be recirculating heat on this sweltering summer night. Alice walked into the living room.

"Hi," Liz said.

Alice set the opened pint bottle of Bacardi rum on the coffee table. A significant portion was missing from the top. "Something you want to talk about?" she asked.

Liz stared at the TV. Boggs hit a grounder to second. Easy out at first. "Rats," she muttered.

"I didn't know you were such a fan," Alice said.

"I'm not," Liz replied, finally looking at her.

Alice pointed at the bottle. "Did our water suddenly go bad just as you were hit by an unquenchable thirst?"

"Alice, I went to Maine today."

"Oh, that explains a lot."

"No, let me finish. So I stopped at the New Hampshire liquor store on the way home, bought some fresh strawberries—"

"At the liquor store?"

"No! Oh, never mind." Liz pressed her head back against the couch. The room was still spinning, but not nearly as badly as before. Liz saw the glass holding the remains of her strawberry daiquiri on the coffee table. The Red Sox had taken the field.

Alice sat down on the couch. "Sorry," she said. "So, how's Maine? Is the ocean still there?" When Liz didn't reply, she said, "Please don't answer, you know how much I enjoy these conversations."

Liz wasn't completely ignoring Alice. She stared at the TV while she tried to force her thoughts into some order. There was something she was forgetting.

"Oh, Alice, I have to tell you!" she said, just then remembering.

"Tell me what?"

"I had dinner at Glenn's last night."

While Alice listened—for once not interrupting—Liz blurted out the story of her evening with Glenn.

Alice whistled softly when she stopped. "This is beginning to be interesting," she said. "But there's one tiny piece of this puzzle still missing. Why did you go to Maine? And please don't tell me you started your afternoon of drinking there or I'll wring your little neck."

"I didn't spend the afternoon drinking! I had one drink!"

The phone rang. Alice reached for it. "Hello," she said, and after a short pause, "Sure." She handed the phone to Liz. "It's for you."

"Hello," Liz said.

"Hi. It's Glenn. How are you?"

"Ah, fine, I guess," Liz said, shocked to hear Glenn's voice.

"Laura told me you left early. I've been worried about you today."

Liz felt something inside herself start to crumble. "Nah, I'm fine," she said, slightly slurring her words.

"Liz, are you okay?"

"Well, yeah. Why?"

"I don't know. I thought—oh, never mind. There's something I'd like to ask you, okay?"

"Sure."

"I was wondering if you'd like to go out on Saturday. We could have dinner, or something."

"On Saturday?" Liz asked, slowly comprehending. "That sounds great. I'd like to."

"Good. Oh, there's one more thing. I want you to take tomorrow off. I've already told Laura not to come in. I'll probably only stay until after lunch myself. Liz," Glenn added, "will you do me a favor? Will you please take care of yourself until Saturday?"

"No problem," Liz answered, grinning broadly.

"That was Glenn," Liz said after she hung up. She stared at the far wall for several seconds, then looked at Alice. "What do you think about that?"

Alice rolled her eyes in a hopeless gesture and said, "I think you have a date."

ChapterEight

Glenn felt a rush of heat sweep through her body when she heard the doorbell ring on Saturday night. She smiled uncertainly and rose to answer it.

"Hello," she said as she swung the door open.

Liz stood on the top step. Glenn caught her breath. Liz was dressed in khaki pants and a soft-colored print shirt; a yellow cotton sweater was slung over one shoulder. Her long hair seemed richly dark, especially in contrast to her pale shirt. But it was seeing her tentative smile and the nervous light in her eyes that made Glenn almost step forward and kiss her—then wonder why she hadn't.

"Hi," Liz said.

"Come on in."

"You look great," Liz said as she stepped through the door.

Glenn glanced at herself. After much debate, she'd chosen a beige silk shirt and black pants. Tight black pants.

"Thanks. So do you." She closed the door.

They walked through the house and out onto the deck. Glenn had to smile as the first moment passed and she felt unable to think of a single thing to say. "I'm glad to see you," she said, speaking honestly.

"Thanks. I'm glad to see you, too."

"So, what did you do yesterday?"

"I slept in. For a while I thought I was going to sleep all day. Alice took a half day off from work, so I went to the beach with her. See my tan?" Liz held up her forearm.

Glenn reached over and brushed her fingers lightly against Liz's skin. "Very impressive," she said. "You must wonder why you're spending your summer indoors when you could be outside being a beach bum." She barely paused before adding, "It seems like a long time since I've seen you."

Liz smiled now. "It does. What did you do today?"

"I spent the morning doing errands," Glenn answered. To herself she added, and I spent the afternoon wondering what I'm getting into with you and how I plan to explain breaking off something that hasn't even started when I leave here to take a job in San Francisco I don't yet have.

"I've made a reservation for us," she said. "Maybe we should go. I hope you like this place."

Glenn had chosen one of her favorite restaurants. She had eaten there many times, with many different women. The restaurant was in an old building; the fragrance from the old wood, the dim lighting and the flickering candles on white linen tablecloths combined to produce an undeniably romantic atmosphere. Glenn never minded being accused of being a romantic.

She and Liz were seated in a large, secluded booth. Glenn reached for the wine list.

"Are you interested in some wine?" she asked, letting her voice rise intentionally with the question.

"Sure," Liz said.

Glenn felt a mischievous impulse overtake her. "If you don't mind my asking, what did you do on Thursday?"

Liz blushed. "I drove to the southern coast of Maine," she stammered. "Sorry I left without telling you. I guess I needed a break."

Glenn watched her, amused. "That's funny. For some reason, I thought you had been drinking when I called."

Liz turned a deeper shade of red. "One drink—I had one strawberry daiquiri." She tried to laugh. "You're as bad as Alice."

"I had lunch with a friend—Pamela—on Thursday," Glenn said. Finally she had told Pam about Liz. "I was surprised when you weren't at work when I got back. So, what made you go running off to the coast of Maine?" she asked, wanting to dig deeper into whatever was causing Liz to feel so embarrassed.

Instant pain showed in Liz's eyes. "Can't we please start with an easier question?"

"Sure. We can talk about anything you want to talk about."

"Good. So how much longer do you think it will be until we finish the project?"

Now Glenn knew the aggrieved look was on her face. "You don't really want to talk about work, do you, Liz?"

"No, I don't want to talk about work. But that's what you always change the subject to when it seems you don't like where a conversation is leading."

"Do I? You're not serious, are you?"

Liz nodded.

"All right, then. I suppose we're even."

Glenn picked up the menu and began scanning through it. By some unspoken agreement they both retreated to safer ground in their conversation. Through dinner Glenn enjoyed just watching Liz. Liz's eyes were bright; occasionally they flashed with excitement. Her voice and other movements seemed weighted with an affected calm. Glenn was glad that her eyes had escaped her guard.

"You didn't grow up around here, did you?" Liz asked when they were nearly finished eating.

"No. I grew up outside of Washington, D.C. How did you know?"

"You're missing the telltale accent. Although I suppose that's no absolute indication that you aren't from around here. Does your family still live there?"

"Yes. My parents both work for the government. I have a younger brother who's a lawyer. He still lives there." Glenn paused before adding, "I don't see them very often any more. We used to be close, but that changed a while ago."

Glenn leaned back against the soft leather of the booth. She intertwined her hands around her wine glass.

"What about you? Where's home for you?"

"In western New York. Near Buffalo. My parents still live there."

"Do you have brothers or sisters?"

"Yes. Two sisters—twins. They're two years older than I am. We used to be close. It seems like we've drifted apart since I've lived here."

"And how long is that?"

Liz stopped to think. "A year and a half."

"Your sisters live near your parents?"

"Yes. They're both married now. Becky already has two kids. Judy just got married this summer. I don't know, being around family, I guess that's just not my style," she ended offhandedly.

Neither said anything for a moment. Then Glenn said, "What *is* your style, Liz?"

Liz blushed and looked away. "I don't know. Maybe taking care of myself, making sure I'm okay."

"That sounds a little lonely."

"Not always. I do all right."

"Liz, I have to tell you something," Glenn said, sensing Liz had begun to feel uncomfortable. "You probably already know by now anyway." She waited until Liz looked up. "I'm very attracted to you. I think you're a very attractive woman."

Liz hesitated. "I feel attracted to you, too."

For a moment neither spoke.

"This has been a crazy couple of weeks, hasn't it?" Glenn said.

"I didn't know what was going on."

"I confused you." Glenn's words were equally a statement and a question.

"Let's just say it seemed like the boundaries were always changing. I knew they were there. I just wasn't always sure where they were."

"I guess you could say we've crossed one boundary just by being here tonight."

Liz nodded.

Glenn lifted her wine glass and swirled the small amount that remained in it. She stared at the rolling liquid then looked at Liz. "Maybe we'll cross another before this night is over."

―――

After dinner they returned to Glenn's house. Inside, Glenn shut and locked the door. Liz watched from a few steps away. Glenn went to her. Not hesitating now, she leaned forward to kiss her, her mouth meeting Liz's, soft and waiting.

Glenn felt Liz's hand on her shoulder. She closed her eyes, relaxing now, losing herself in the feel of Liz's mouth finally pressing against hers.

When Glenn opened her eyes, she saw Liz looking at her. She stepped back, but her eyes lingered on Liz and she felt Liz leaning closer, still wanting her. "I've wanted to do that for a very long time," Glenn said softly.

"So have I."

Glenn glanced over Liz's shoulder at the couch. She started to suggest they sit there, but other words came out when she spoke. "Why don't we go upstairs?"

Liz nodded and followed Glenn when she moved towards the stairway.

"I suppose I shouldn't be surprised, but I am," Liz said in an awed voice when they reached the bedroom. "This room is beautiful." She walked towards the balcony.

Glenn came over and stood behind her. She put her arms around Liz, joining them at her waist. She smiled when she felt Liz jump.

"How are you doing, Liz?"

Liz turned; a smile spread slowly over her face. "I'm doing fine."

Glenn took Liz's hand and led her to the bed. Lying close, Glenn felt a crazy swelling of excitement and anticipation. Liz moved towards her; Glenn felt their lips touching, her mouth opening, and Liz's tongue inside, meeting hers in long, sensuous strokes. Glenn reached behind and stroked Liz's back beneath her shirt—touching her for the first time. She moved her hand higher, caressing her warm skin in light touches.

Liz broke their kiss. She moved back, then shivered as Glenn's fingers moved to her side, near her breast.

Glenn smiled. "Now isn't this exactly where you always thought you and I would end up?"

"Thought? No."

"But you wanted this."

"Yes, I've wanted it."

"So have I."

"Then why did you throw me out on Wednesday night?" Liz demanded, pretending to feel annoyed.

"Is that why you ran away on Thursday?"

Liz lowered her eyes, embarrassed again. "Well, maybe there was some connection."

"Liz, I wasn't ready—"

Glenn broke off when she felt Liz's mouth moving against hers. Unexpected joy surged inside her to know Liz wanted this as much as she did. Liz's hand was on the top button of her shirt. It remained there. Liz broke the kiss and moved back slightly.

"Do you mind?" she asked as she twisted the button free.

"No," Glenn answered in an unusually husky voice. Tears glistened in her eyes, but she doubted Liz would notice them.

Liz slowly loosed each of the buttons. When she finished she leaned over, letting her lips brush against Glenn's breast.

Intense pleasure coursed through Glenn. She closed her eyes and stretched her head back. Liz's lips and tongue moved over her breast, teasing her nipple, then moved to her other breast and caused the whole wave of sensations to start over.

Glenn gasped softly when she felt Liz's hand move lower, brushing over her pants. Liz tugged at the zipper. Glenn caught her breath when she felt Liz sliding her hand beneath her pants. Liz smiled at her, but she still teased her, drawing her fingers in sensuous lines over the thin fabric of her underwear, then lifting it, slipping underneath.

Glenn felt warmth and wetness flooding, betraying her desire. Liz was watching her. For one instant Glenn felt terrified by their connection—by this hold Liz had on her, the way she touched her, her fingers, even now, exciting her more.

"Let's get undressed," Glenn said faintly. She moved to sit up, to start unbuttoning Liz's shirt.

When they were both undressed, Liz lay flat against the white sheet. Glenn dared to steal long moments before she looked away, not wanting Liz to become self-conscious. Then bolder, she sat up. She stroked Liz's flat belly and her soft breasts, she saw her nipples already erect. Glenn brushed her fingers over her dark pubic hair, smiling when Liz quivered. She moved lower, to her thighs, stroking her firm muscles, drawing her finger across the brown tan line on her thigh, touching her legs, wanting to touch her everywhere.

Suddenly Glenn couldn't wait any longer. She stretched full-length beside Liz and tentatively reached between her legs. Liz moaned softly, but she didn't resist. Glenn began teasing her, lightly. She felt Liz's clitoris, then traced over it. Then she slipped lower, hesitating, before sliding inside Liz.

"Talk to me, Liz," she whispered. "Tell me what you want."

Liz opened her eyes, looking more vulnerable, more exposed, than Glenn had ever seen her.

"Everything—it feels great," she answered softly, her breath coming in short gasps.

Glenn smiled tenderly. "No. You tell me when it's really good."

Glenn held her hand firmly inside Liz, hardly moving, then moving so slightly it was as if she wasn't moving at all. She smiled when she felt Liz's body rising against her. Slowly, Glenn withdrew her hand. Liz gasped softly. But Glenn began rubbing harder and quicker, sliding over her clitoris then slipping inside her again.

"Yes," Liz cried. "That's it."

Glenn repeated the motion, wanting to remember it. She alternated, inside and out, teasing and stroking until she heard Liz cry loudly. Still holding her inside, Glenn felt the unmistakable spasm of Liz's vagina quickening, her body relaxing gradually.

Glenn gently coaxed Liz until she looked at her. "That doesn't usually happen to me the first time I make love with someone," Liz finally said.

"I'm glad it happened tonight."

For one brief, ill-considered moment Glenn thought she was so happy she didn't care whether Liz made love to her. As soon as Liz started touching her, Glenn knew it mattered very much. Her body swelled quickly with excitement. When Liz moved between her legs and slid towards the end of the bed, Glenn knew immediately what she intended. Liz moved closer until Glenn felt her tongue pressing into her.

Glenn heard herself cry out. Liz's tongue was warm and soft, exciting her intensely. Then Liz's fingers were inside her. Time stopped, and Glenn felt wave after wave rush through her. Liz played with her body. She repeated a pattern of movement, seemingly endlessly; then she ceased all movement, held herself still, then slowly began stroking her again. Glenn gasped for breath. She gave up trying to predict what Liz would do next. Her body yielded completely to Liz's touch.

Out of the haze of sensation Glenn felt something strike and hold inside. It deepened and swelled, sending out ripples. Glenn heard herself moaning loudly. Liz repeated the same rhythmical motion. In a slow, lazy sort of way Glenn felt her body rising towards orgasm. Then it broke. Acute release flooded through her, her vagina contracting in wave after wave.

Liz moved to lie next to her. Glenn waited a moment, then looked at her. "Where did you learn to make love like that?" she blurted before adding, "Never mind. My god, Liz, that was wonderful."

Liz seemed both embarrassed and pleased.

Glenn took a deep breath. Her head was straight back on the pillow, and she stared at the ceiling. Then she looked at Liz, touching the few strands of hair that as usual had fallen forward. Her eyes had softened, but her voice still had the sound of breathlessness in it when she spoke. "God, I'm happy to be with you."

———

Glenn awoke the next morning to see light pouring in through the windows. She had no idea what time it was. Liz, lying beside her, was still sleeping.

Memories of the night before startled Glenn out of the last of her drowsiness. She rolled onto her side and brushed Liz's cheek.

Liz's eyes opened. "Good morning," she said. Her mouth opened wide into a yawn.

"Good morning, sleepyhead. Did you sleep well?"

"Yes, and for your information, I was awake once already this morning."

"Oh, then why didn't you wake me?"

"I was being kind."

"I see." Glenn leaned over to kiss her.

Glenn was surprised when she looked at a clock to see that it was already after eleven. Downstairs, she made coffee and brought in the Sunday paper. She joined Liz on the deck.

Liz was leaning with her head back against the chair, gazing out over the lake. She cradled her coffee cup with both hands. Glenn watched her for a moment, then looked out at the lake where a dozen bright sails were flapping high above small boats.

"Well, I guess I should get going," Liz said a short time later.

Glenn looked up in surprise. "Why? Do you have plans for today?"

"Well, no. I thought maybe you had things you needed to do."

Glenn smiled. Ordinarily she was relieved to part company with her previous night's date. "No, I don't have anything planned. I was hoping you could stay."

Liz relaxed in her chair. "Thanks. Actually, I'd like to."

After they finished eating breakfast and reading the paper, they walked down to the water's edge and sat on the dock. Though Glenn offered to lend her a bathing suit, Liz contented herself with dangling her feet in the water and splashing Glenn.

"I forget how nice it is down here," Glenn said. She was lying full length on the wooden boards.

"You don't spend much time down here?"

"No. Not unless I have company, usually."

Liz was quiet for a moment. "And that doesn't happen often?"

Glenn speculated on what Liz was asking. Finally she said, "If you're asking whether I go out much, the answer is I haven't recently. If you're asking something else, you'll have to be more specific."

Liz turned around and grinned. "My question is answered, thank you very much."

"I suppose I shouldn't tell you this, but it's been a long time since I've enjoyed being with someone as much as I've enjoyed being with you."

Liz rolled over to lie on her stomach. "And why shouldn't I know that?"

"Because there's no telling what you'll ask me next and what I'll find myself telling you!"

"That sounds like a terrible fate. Am I ever so untrustworthy?"

"I don't know. Are you?"

"Untrustworthy? Not at all. Actually, I'm a safe bet."

"Hmm, I wonder. Which reminds me—I've told you the status of my love life. What about yours?"

"Nonexistent."

"I find that hard to believe." Glenn rolled onto her side and reached over to stroke Liz's arm.

"It's true. It's been over a year since I've been involved with anyone."

"A year? That's funny. It was a year ago when I broke up with Diana." Glenn paused, then added, "Diana used to live here. But that's another story. I was certain you were involved with Alice."

Liz laughed. "No. Alice and I are very good friends and we prefer to keep it that way. I don't know, I guess until recently I didn't know anyone who I wanted to go out with."

"Liz, are you always so indirect?" Glenn asked, hurt by her nonchalance.

Liz stopped smiling. "I am when I'm not sure of myself," she said, then added, "Sorry." She sat up and looked out across the water.

The wind had started blowing. It caught her hair, pulling the long strands in all directions. Glenn sat up and reached over to brush her hair away from her eyes.

Turning to her, Liz said, "I was attracted to you practically from the first moment I saw you, believe it or not. I've spent a lot of weeks wondering about you, but I never thought for one minute that anything might happen between us. This is a fairly big change in our relationship."

"I think so, too. Which leads me to say, I would very much like to see you again. It worries me to think we have to work together, though."

Liz smiled. "Don't worry, I won't be a liability to you. Discretion is an art I've learned to practice."

Glenn laughed and said, "I'm not really worried. I guess I just had to say that. Let's go back up to the house," she continued. "Discretion is not something I'm interested in practicing right now."

Chapter Nine

Monday morning Liz sat at her desk jotting down a few last minute notes before breaking from her work to go to a meeting. Laura interrupted her.

"Haven't seen you all morning. Working hard?"

"Yes. I've been here since seven." Liz stretched her arms above her head and barely held back a yawn.

Laura walked in and sat down. "You didn't work on Friday, did you?"

"No."

"Me neither. Thank god we finally got a break. What did you do this weekend?"

Liz felt a rush of panic. The question was innocent; Laura had said the same thing every Monday for the last eight weeks. "Not much," she replied, falsely calm. "I went to the beach on Friday. Other than that, nothing special. What about you?"

"Rick and I visited friends. Yesterday we looked at houses. Expensive houses. I think going through houses we like but can't afford is our civilized way of torturing each other."

"I guess we'd better go," Liz said, looking at her watch. "Glenn's probably waiting."

Status meetings had become a ritual for the three of them in recent weeks. Liz listened while Glenn questioned Laura about her work. Their words floated to her ears, but this morning she paid little attention. She sat quietly, staring at the sheet of paper in her hands.

Liz felt more uncomfortable than she'd expected, being this close to Glenn. This morning Glenn seemed more a stranger than either the project manager she had known for weeks or the woman she had made love with yesterday. And Laura—Liz felt new panic, thinking Laura might know she and Glenn were lovers. It was a crazy thought. She forced it from her mind.

"Your turn," Liz heard Glenn say. She looked up. "So where are you with your work?"

"Oh. I finished the file purge program this morning and I'm almost done with the backup and restore piece. They're small. I should finish today."

Glenn nodded and turned to her own notes. "In that case, it looks like we'll finish phase two by tomorrow. That's the good news. The bad news is that we're running out of time. I had planned to do a unit test of phase two just as we did for phase one, but now I think I'll have you both move on to phase three and we'll test everything at the end. That could be as early as next week. Do either of you have any objections to that?"

Liz and Laura shook their heads no.

"All right then, I only have one more thing to say. And that is, nobody works any more overtime around here. I mean it. The schedule goes before either of you lose your health or your mind over this. And if we don't finish before you return to school," she added, looking at Liz, "you simply will be forbidden to leave until we do!"

Liz laughed and looked down. For one instant her mind flashed back to her first weeks at Allied Industries, a time she hadn't thought of for weeks. Now, the contrast in Glenn's behavior struck her sharply.

Late in the afternoon Liz found an excuse to see Glenn alone.

"Are you playing soccer tonight?" Glenn asked.

"Yes. We're playing against the team we played when I first hurt my ankle."

"Don't tell me these things!" Glenn said softly, her tone one of mock horror.

Liz just smiled.

"Where are you playing?"

"At our home field, Ashbury Middle School. Do you want to come and watch?"

"And see you get mangled? I don't think so. Will you call me later?"

"Sure."

That night Liz came off of the field just before the first half ended and was surprised to see Glenn standing on the sidelines.

"Hello," she said. "I didn't expect to see you here."

"Well, I changed my mind. Who's winning?"

"No score yet."

The referee's whistle sounded in a loud screech; the first half was over. Liz turned to look for Alice, then signaled to her when she caught her eye.

"I've heard about you," Alice said to Glenn after Liz had introduced them. "Thinking of joining this team?"

Before Glenn had a chance to reply, Jeanne called the team together for a halftime meeting. When she finished, Alice leaned towards Liz and whispered, "Did anyone ever tell you you have remarkable taste in women, Edwards?"

Liz laughed. "No one ever had to."

The meeting broke up and the two teams returned to the field. For the first ten minutes neither team could gain any advantage over the other. Finally Liz received a clean pass with no opponent near her. She ran for a few steps, then kicked the ball from her position near the sidelines across and into the center of the field. As the ball came off her foot, Liz lunged forward, all of her weight going down onto her right foot. The weak ankle buckled beneath her when she landed on the hard ground.

Liz never saw the goal Jeanne scored. She heard the excited cheers of her teammates and was vaguely aware of what had happened. Alice rushed over to her.

"Nice cross," Alice said, kneeling down. "I believe that's called an assist for you."

"Thanks. Can I have a hand?"

"My pleasure."

With Alice's help, Liz hobbled to the sidelines. Someone brought her ice. Glenn found a towel to wrap around her leg.

"I was hoping you wouldn't make me sorry I came," Glenn said. "Is this what always happens?"

Liz felt dizzy; her ankle hurt worse than usual. "I don't know," she said, unsure what Glenn had asked. She leaned forward, hoping to clear her head.

"Are you okay?" Glenn asked.

Liz shut her eyes tightly. Remembering Glenn, she tried to speak coherently. "Yes. I think I just need some water."

"So, tell me," Glenn pursued after Liz drank cold water, "is this what always happens when you play soccer?"

"Not always. Lately—yes." Liz reached down to adjust the ice pack on her leg. She was sick of always reinjuring her ankle during games. "I think I won't play again for a while. Summer season's almost over anyway."

"And I think that's good news," Glenn said.

The score remained 1-0 through the rest of the game. By the time it ended, Liz was feeling well enough to stand. Her teammates gathered on the sidelines and everyone exchanged words of congratulations.

"Can I give you a ride home?" Glenn asked as the women began wandering away.

"Well, I've got my car—"

"No problem. I'll drive it home for you," Alice said, appearing at that moment. "I want to stop and celebrate this momentous victory anyway. How are you feeling?" she asked, clearly an afterthought.

"Terrific. I was thinking about going out for a run tonight. Would you like to come with me?"

"No thanks. But I will look for you in the emergency room tomorrow morning. No doubt you'll be in traction by then. If you ask me, that's the perfect place for you."

Liz just glared at her, unwilling to speculate whether Alice intended a hidden message.

"So, what am I going to have to do to get an invitation to spend the night with you?" Glenn asked while they were driving back into the city.

"You've got it," Liz said, hiding her surprise.

Liz showered quickly once they were home. She walked into the living room to find Tex, Alice's small gray cat, sitting beside Glenn and purring madly.

"Does this funny little cat belong to you?" Glenn asked.

"Tex belongs to Alice. He's her longest relationship."

"I like Alice."

"She's a good one," Liz agreed.

"How's your ankle feeling?"

Liz sat down on the couch next to Glenn. "It's not great, but it's not as bad as it's been before."

"Has it ever occurred to you that soccer is a dangerous game?" Glenn asked.

"Until recently—no."

"Well it has occurred to me. You make me nervous, running around on that field."

Liz shrugged. "Our season is almost over. I won't try to play again until the fall."

Glenn moved closer and put one arm around her. Liz felt strangely uncomfortable sitting so close to Glenn in her own living room. She didn't think it was likely that Alice would be home any time soon, but she couldn't be sure. She felt suddenly shy about having Alice see her and Glenn together.

"Do you want to go into my room?" she asked as soon as she could change the subject.

"I thought you'd never ask," Glenn teased.

They went into the bedroom and lay down together. Liz felt a moment's disbelief to see Glenn lying on her bed. Hadn't this been her dream, her fantasy? She moved closer to kiss Glenn. Quickly, she lost herself in the feeling of Glenn's mouth pressing against hers.

"And what kind of day did you have?" she said when she broke their kiss.

"A very long one," Glenn replied. She rolled onto her back and inhaled a deep breath. "But this is my favorite part, so far."

Liz laughed and leaned over to kiss her again. She brushed back the curl from Glenn's forehead though it fell immediately back into place; she was warmed by the sparkle in Glenn's eyes. Glenn put her hands behind Liz's head and held her there.

"You're really something, do you know that?" Glenn said.

Embarrassed, Liz smiled, but she didn't reply.

"You surprise me all the time," Glenn continued. "You're smart, and funny, and beautiful, and wonderful to make love with, and—" Glenn stopped. "And what I like best is that I can embarrass you so easily."

Liz gave a short laugh.

"I can't imagine that one of those women on your team hasn't caught up with you before now."

"Well, none has," Liz replied, still uncomfortable.

Liz put her hand on Glenn's waist and leaned over, gently moving her hand across Glenn's body while they kissed again. Glenn reached to Liz's shirt and began unbuttoning it. Liz sat back as Glenn moved from one button down to the next. Then Glenn reached in to stroke her skin. Liz quivered violently despite the gentleness of Glenn's touch.

Liz breathed quietly and moved to stretch out flat on her back. She felt Glenn moving her fingers in long, seductive circles over her stomach, finding her ribs, reaching for her breasts. Liz felt a quiet scream explode inside her when Glenn touched one breast, held it, then reached for the other. Glenn smiled. She drew open Liz's shirt and leaned over to kiss her.

❀

Glenn read through the informal note she had just written to Ann Carlyle in San Francisco. She frowned, then read it again, wondering why she didn't just say she was no longer interested in any job. Her polite inquiry implied interest. But if I was really interested, I'd just call, she admitted. She sealed the note in an envelope and left it on the kitchen counter to mail the next day.

It was late, but Glenn walked into the living room and sat down for a few minutes anyway. She wished she had thought to turn on some music. But she didn't intend to stay up long. It had been such a pleasant night, she hated for it to end. Glenn laughed shortly and wondered when the last time was that she could say that about an evening alone with Diana.

They had had dinner together. It was their first chance to talk alone in recent months. Though she had spoken briefly of her plans to move, it had been clear the subject was hard for them both. So they had avoided it. Diana had had dozens of new stories to tell, anyway. Glenn smiled pensively. Tonight she had felt only affection for Diana—not even a twinge of anger.

Glenn leaned her head against the soft fabric of the sofa and wondered what was different. She wondered if Liz was the difference. Though she hadn't mentioned Liz to Diana, she had thought of her often during the evening—felt her, rather—in waves of warmth flooding through her at the tiniest recollection of their new relationship.

"I saw Diana the other night," Glenn said to Liz when they were together the following Thursday night.

"Oh," Liz said, looking up, a neutral, yet slightly guarded, look in her eyes.

Glenn left the windows where she had been watching the summer drizzle misting on the glass. "I guess some old feelings and memories were stirred up. I've been thinking about her since then."

Glenn watched Liz carefully as she walked closer, curious how she would react to hearing about Diana.

Abruptly, Liz asked, "Is there any chance you and Diana might get back together?"

Glenn smiled reassuringly, yet she felt a trace of reserve lingering in her expression. "No. There's no chance of that." She sank onto the sofa next to Liz. "Diana is happily involved with a woman named Joyce. As for me, too much has changed for me to ever feel the same about her."

"But you still see her?"

"Actually, I see her pretty often. We're still quite close, if you can believe that."

Glenn felt surprised when she realized she wanted to tell Liz about Diana. She hadn't planned to dig up that story tonight. For one moment she thought she would ignore her impulse; then, just as impulsively, she asked, "Do you mind if I tell you about Diana?"

"No," Liz answered, her expression again neutral, concealing any uncertainty she still felt.

"I don't talk about the past very much any more," Glenn started, almost apologetic. "I think I talked about Diana for so long I got sick of hearing myself. For some reason I feel like telling you about her." She paused to look at Liz, then relaxed, resting her head back against the soft cushions behind her.

"I was in love with Diana. I felt as though I had met the woman with whom I wanted to spend the rest of my life. We met four years ago, fell madly in love, and eventually moved into this house. Diana worked with the architect on the design of the house; it is the way it is because she wanted it that way.

"Things between us were great for two years after we started living together, then fell apart badly in the third year. I guess I wanted the relationship to work out, so I tended to see only the good things we had. Diana's unhappiness and frustration were greater, so she saw only the bad. We started having terrible fights—often over little things." Glenn sighed tiredly. "I know I'm not an angel—that I can have quite a bad temper. But I couldn't believe how angry Diana could get. She would become so stone-faced and rigid—completely withdrawn—and there was nothing I could say or do to get through to her!"

Unexpectedly, Glenn felt shaken by her memories. Diana hadn't lived in this house for over a year, but Glenn could feel her presence now. She could almost see her sitting in the leather ottoman, leafing through financial reports as she had done on so many nights. Glenn had insisted Diana take the ottoman, along with nearly all of their other furniture. Replacing household goods, however expensive, had been the least she could do to attempt to recreate a home for herself.

"I suppose Diana, in her own way, tried to tell me that our ideas about the relationship were different. She claims she tried to tell me that this was not the relationship she imagined staying involved in over a lifetime. I don't know now whether she did or didn't. If she did, maybe I just didn't want to hear it.

"Diana works as an investment advisor. A little more than a year ago she attended a conference in New York and was gone for a few days. When she returned, she told me she had met someone else, someone with whom she wanted to get involved.

"I was stunned. That night was the last we spent together. Diana moved out the next day. Several days later she started seeing Joyce." Glenn smiled weakly. "It's funny. Diana loves being near the water. The fact that she moved out just when it was getting nice here made me know how serious she was about breaking up."

Glenn was quiet for a moment. "In spite of everything, I do have to give Diana credit, though. I believe she was as kind to me as she could have been, under the circumstances. She didn't waver in her decision to leave me, and she didn't get involved with Joyce until after she moved. And she insisted that I continue to live here."

"I can't believe you were friends through all of that," Liz exclaimed when Glenn stopped.

"Oh, we weren't friends at the time. We didn't start seeing each other again for months. I think that was the lowest point in my life. I'm still not sure how I got through it. The truth was I didn't want to have anything to do with Diana, and I certainly didn't want to know Joyce. Seeing them both was fairly unavoidable, though." Glenn looked at Liz, half shrugging. "We had the same friends. More than that, Diana was determined that we should be friends." Glenn hesitated, feeling her eyes suddenly set hard. "And what Diana wants, she usually gets. I don't know, I think Diana always valued our friendship more than she did anything else in our relationship."

"Do you feel that you've gotten over her?" Liz asked.

Glenn laughed more easily. "Yes, I am relieved to say that I have. Although I know I'll always feel very strongly about her and about that time in my life. Last fall I started dating again, but I haven't become seriously involved with anyone. Maybe I'm not quite as ready for that as I think I am."

Suddenly Liz said, "So all of this was going on last summer, when you had the problem at work?"

"Yes." Glenn sighed deeply. "Diana moved out just before everything fell apart there. My whole world seemed to be caving in more each day. I had already lost my lover; I nearly lost my job. If I'd been fired, I don't know whether I would have been able to keep this house. Can you imagine what would have happened to me then?"

Liz shook her head.

"Would you like to see a picture of Diana?" Glenn asked.

"Sure."

Glenn got up and walked over to the bookcase. She removed a photograph, inserted between two books.

"She's beautiful," Liz exclaimed.

"Yes, she is," Glenn agreed. She looked at the picture in Liz's hands. The image exuded health and well-being. Diana's features—the clear skin in her oval-shaped face, the thin line of her nose, her long brown hair, her shining brown eyes—were the features of classic American beauty.

Glenn said, "Diana is one of those rare individuals who seem to have it all: beauty, intelligence, education, wealth. Her family has been wealthy for generations. It doesn't seem fair. Not that she's perfect, either."

"That seems a little hard to believe at the moment," Liz said softly.

Glenn looked at Liz and wondered if she felt intimidated either by Diana or by what she had said about their relationship. She put her arm around her and held her closely. "Diana's personality runs hot and cold. She can be very kind and loving, and she can just as easily be cold and mean. I was never very good at dealing with her changing moods. All I ever wanted was to lose myself in her, to yield to her and not be responsible for my own life. Since breaking up I've had to learn to take care of myself and that's been a good thing, much as I hate to admit it. I never want to be that dependent on anyone again."

"It's hard for me to imagine you being dependent on anyone."

Glenn laughed. "I'm not as tough as I sometimes want people to think I am."

"Like me, for example?" Liz asked.

"No, not like you, for example." Glenn leaned over and kissed her. "With you I can just be myself."

Glenn rested her head on Liz's shoulder.

"Do you want to go away on Saturday?" she asked. "I have a party to go to tomorrow night, but other than that, my weekend is free."

"You're not worried about someone from work seeing us together?"

Glenn smiled and said, "I'm willing to take that chance."

❀

"So, tell me," Pamela said, rushing over when Glenn entered the crowded room for Sara's party, "what's happening with your office romance? I called you the other night—didn't you get my message?"

"Yes, I got your message," Glenn answered. "And I did call you back, but you weren't home." Glenn smiled at Marie and Eve, who had caught her eye from across the room.

"Glenn! You went out last weekend?" Pamela asked impatiently.

"Yes. On Saturday."

"And?"

"And we had a very good time. Liz stayed Saturday night," Glenn added, knowing Pamela would ask anyway.

"And?"

"And we had great sex," Glenn replied, in exasperation giving her stock answer.

"Of course," Pamela said, "you always do. Now tell me something different about this new affair of yours."

"Well," Glenn said, laughter in her eyes, "I've seen her twice since then. And we're going away tomorrow."

"That is different," Pamela exclaimed. "So tell me, where do you think all of this is leading?"

"All of what?" Diana asked, just then joining them.

Pamela didn't say anything.

"Oh," Glenn said, "Pamela is just trying to figure out how serious I am about a woman I've started seeing. Her ulterior motives are fairly transparent."

"So how serious are you?" Diana asked. "And why didn't you tell me about her on Tuesday?"

Pamela excused herself, and Diana and Glenn walked outside.

"I didn't say anything because there wasn't much to say. I've been seeing her for less than a week!"

"Is she the one who was at your house the night I called?" Diana asked.

"Yes. Although we weren't involved at that point. The complication has been that she works for me."

"She must be something to have managed to get your attention within the walls of Allied Industries."

"She is."

"Why didn't she come with you tonight?"

"I didn't invite her." Seeing the questioning expression on Diana's face, Glenn continued, "And feed her to you sharks? No, that wouldn't have been kind." Glenn knew her friends well enough to know that, had Liz been with her, they both would have been subjected to endless scrutiny by Pamela, Diana and the others, all trying to determine how serious their relationship was.

"Glenn, you exaggerate!" Diana said, using her sweetest voice. "We would have behaved ourselves."

Glenn laughed and shook her head in disbelief.

"Well, I'll tell you what then. Why don't you two come over for dinner next Saturday. I'll invite Pam, and one or two others. It will be a small group. No sharks."

Glenn shook her head, not wanting to consent to this plan.

"Joyce will cook," Diana said.

"Does Joyce know anything about this?"

"Of course, we've been planning something like this for months. Now that we have a date, it's settled. Will you come?"

"I'll see," Glenn said, conceding just barely. "Diana," she continued, "did anyone ever tell you that you're a manipulator?"

"Yes—you," Diana replied.

———

Glenn knew her friends had the best intentions in trying to encourage her in this new relationship. The effect of their unrestrained interest, however, only caused her to ask herself new, and harder, questions about the time she was spending with Liz. She fell asleep late Friday night, worried that she was getting involved too fast in a relationship she wasn't sure she wanted to be involved in at all.

Saturday morning she awoke feeling rested and, unexpectedly, anxious to see Liz. While packing her few things to go away she repeated the warnings she had given herself the night before: she had to move slowly in whatever was happening with Liz. Undeniably, she felt torn. Still, her first decision had to be whether she was moving to the West Coast. Though she hadn't worried about it lately, moving was still bound to be a wrenching ordeal. Neither she nor Liz needed the complication of an involved relationship to make the experience any worse.

Just before noon she and Liz arrived at the women's guest house on the Cape where Glenn had made a reservation. They changed into swimming suits and beach clothes then picked up sandwiches in town.

The woman at the guest house had suggested a smaller, less popular beach a few miles outside of town. They found it without difficulty. Glenn and Liz spread their blanket out on a secluded spot. Glenn collapsed on it, enjoying the feel of the sun's rays soaking into her, already feeling more relaxed than she had in many days. Liz, also, seemed glad for the chance to unwind. Through the afternoon they talked only a little.

"Did you enjoy the party last night?" Liz asked at dinner that night.

"Yes," Glenn replied. "I had a good time." She started to say more but stopped herself. Liz waited expectantly, then lowered her eyes when it was clear Glenn didn't intend to continue.

Suddenly Glenn felt angry with herself. All day she had spoken only of trivial, unimportant matters. Having decided to be careful in what she told Liz about herself, she now found even ordinary thoughts suspect. Atypically, she could think of precious little to say.

The silence was growing; Glenn tried to think how to break it. There was something she wanted to know, she considered uneasily, then decided to plunge forward and ask.

"Well," she said, "in the last week or so I've told you a fair amount about myself, but so far I don't know very much about you."

"What would you like to know?"

Glenn leaned over the table. Twisting her wine glass in one hand, she said, "Tell me about the women in your life."

"Well, all right." Glenn saw a nervous flicker cross Liz's eyes before she took a deep breath, and said, "I've been involved in three more or less serious relationships. The first was when I was a sophomore in college. It didn't last very long, but I learned a lot while I was in it. The second was with someone named Chris. We lived together for a while."

"How long?"

"A little over a year."

"When was that?"

"We broke up almost two years ago. That was before I moved to Boston—when I was still in Syracuse. The third was with a woman named Eileen. We did have a good relationship. Our problem was that we didn't have much in common."

Liz had succeeded in capturing Glenn's interest. "Tell me more," she said when Liz stopped.

"I don't know what else to say," Liz said, shrugging her shoulders. "I stopped seeing Eileen early last summer. Since then, not much has happened in that area of my life."

"What about Chris?" Glenn asked. "You must have had a serious relationship to have decided to live together."

"One of us did. The other didn't, at least not when it mattered."

"That sounds puzzling."

Liz laughed uneasily. "Ours turned out to be a very complicated relationship. The good times we shared didn't last very long. We had a lot of problems. Unfortunately, neither of us knew how to end a relationship."

"What kind of problems?"

"Oh, for one thing, we weren't very good about expressing our feelings. The real problem, though, was that Chris wasn't in love with me. She did try to tell me that. But then she would never let me go either."

"Why did you stay?"

"I didn't know any better," Liz said softly.

"Chris loved someone else?"

"Yes. No." Liz groaned. "There were other women, and there was always her work, which I think she loved more than any person. I wanted her to want me more than she did either her work or the other women. I guess that's why I stayed."

"How did it end?"

"Very badly. We finally moved to separate apartments but kept insisting we would remain friends. Chris didn't want to deal with me, or with her guilt, or with anything that had gone on between us. Pretending nothing had happened seemed easiest. So, we both did that."

Glenn frowned to hear these words. This decimation of love sounded horrible. She could not imagine Liz, whom she knew only to be warm, kind and full of loving feelings, involved in such a barren relationship.

"Liz," she said, "are you telling me that you ended up walking away from a relationship in which you did not share your feelings with your lover and that afterwards neither of you acknowledged that anything important had happened? This, with someone with whom you lived for over a year?"

Glenn expected Liz to say no; she was certain she had misunderstood. When Liz nodded, Glenn was stunned.

They had finished eating. Glenn flagged down the inattentive waiter, they paid the bill and left the restaurant. Walking in the warm night air Glenn tried to imagine what this relationship had been for Liz. She felt troubled by Liz's pained silence and by her feeble attempt to appear at ease.

"Were you so in love with Chris?" she asked abruptly.

"No! Not at the end, anyway."

"Then why did you stay with her?"

Liz didn't reply. She was walking rapidly now; Glenn had to rush to keep pace with her. Finally, in an obvious attempt to sum up the situation blandly, Liz said, "It was a difficult relationship. Some things about it I don't understand. Mostly when I think about it I just remember how angry I was."

"Was?"

Liz shook her head. "Yes, was."

Glenn touched Liz's arm and stopped walking. They were standing outside the guest house where they were staying. She said, "Tell me you're not angry now, Liz."

Liz, in an uncharacteristic move, turned sharply and walked up the steps.

Glenn felt puzzled and confused. Liz stood sulking at the door of their room. Inside, she walked over to the window, not having bothered to turn on the light. Looking at her, Glenn saw only a silhouette, Liz's back and shoulders dark against the scant light showing from the street.

Liz seemed to recover. "I'm sorry, I really am. I don't mean to be difficult."

"Liz, it's okay." Glenn came up behind and put her arms around her. "Nobody ever said that emotions are supposed to be reasonable things."

"I want mine to be. I only want to forget everything that happened with Chris. I didn't need for any of that to happen!"

"Oh, but you probably did," Glenn said warmly, trying to lift her from her black mood. "Someday you may know why."

Liz continued to look through the window to the shadowed street below. Her tone was softer when she spoke. "Sometimes I think I had to learn all of the wrong ways in the world of having a relationship before I would be willing to try and learn the right ways."

"See there—that's worth something."

"Please, spare me," Liz said, her voice rising slightly to give an exaggerated effect to her words. She turned around. A thin smile had replaced the dark expression on her face.

"Just this once," Glenn said.

Sunday night, Glenn sat alone in her living room. She had dropped Liz off at her apartment hours earlier. They had had a wonderful weekend, despite the impasse they had reached on Saturday night. It had been all well and good to ask Liz about her past, Glenn thought, still disturbed by their conversation the night before, but Liz seemed not to have been ready to talk—though why, Glenn didn't know. Her most significant relationship had ended nearly two years ago.

Glenn kicked the coffee table lightly, feeling her forehead crease into a frown. Had she put too much pressure on Liz? Badgering her certainly hadn't been her intention. She really wanted to hear what Liz had to say.

Nice try, she whispered, knowing that wasn't the whole truth. Yes, she had wanted to hear Liz talk about her past, but more than that, asking Liz to talk about herself had struck her as an easy solution to not wanting to draw attention to her own reluctance to talk.

Glenn stopped kicking the table and stared across the room. She had almost said it yesterday. In the afternoon, while she and Liz were lying on the beach, she had almost blurted it out: Liz, I may be moving to San Francisco.

Wouldn't everything be easier if she had?

No, Glenn answered emphatically. This was her decision to make. Fair or not, her decision had to be for what was best for her life, not what was best for her and Liz. Anyway, who knew how long she and Liz would even want to go on seeing each other?

Glenn listened to her silent inner voice, to its earnest effort to persuade, but she knew she didn't believe either her or Liz's feelings would soon fade—or that she had any excuse for not being honest with Liz about her plans.

Chapter Ten

Liz paced unhappily late Tuesday afternoon. Bored by her circle through the department, she wandered downstairs to the cafeteria. What she really wanted was to try to talk to Glenn. But why bother, she asked herself miserably. For two days Glenn had barely noticed she was alive—much less remembered they were lovers. Testing—all Glenn would talk about was the project test scheduled for later this week! Liz knew it might easily be the end of the week before Glenn got back to normal—assuming the project test was really what was causing her so much stress.

Back in the department, Liz couldn't resist stopping at Glenn's office. "You look like you could use a break," she said quietly.

Glenn barely shrugged. "You did a nice job setting up the new test environment. That's going to be great to have, regardless of what happens with the new method."

Before Liz had a chance to respond, Glenn abruptly threw her hands in the air and said, "Do you know what Bob said at the meeting this morning?"

Liz shook her head no.

"He's already told other people in the company what we're trying to do. I can't believe it! Now if this new method doesn't work, I'll only look bad—again. I hate it! This job is like quicksand. All I ever do is fight against sinking deeper."

Liz smiled weakly, hating it that Glenn was still shutting her out.

———

At home that evening Liz flipped through the TV guide listlessly. She wished Alice was home; at the moment she didn't have a clue where Alice might be or whom she might be with. Liz dreaded another night alone. Last night she had talked to Glenn briefly, but other than that they hadn't seen each other since the weekend, except at work.

When the phone rang, Liz felt a wild rush of hope that it might be Glenn. It was.

"Hi. I wanted to apologize for being in such a lousy mood today," Glenn said.

Liz slouched into the couch and put her feet on the coffee table. "Oh, that's all right. Bob must have been a pain at the meeting this morning."

"That's Bob," Glenn said flatly. "Is it hot at your place tonight?"

It was—it always was in the summer—but Liz didn't want to miss a chance for Glenn to come here, if that was why she was asking. "It's not too bad. Why?"

"I thought if you were boiling there you might want to drive out to my place. Sorry I didn't ask you before. I could have saved you a trip."

The sun was just setting when Liz reached Glenn's, but it seemed only slightly cooler here than it had in the city. Liz was disappointed to find Glenn just as tense as she had been all day at work.

"Did you bring your bathing suit?" Glenn asked after refusing Liz's offer of a back rub.

Liz had. She went upstairs to put it on; then she left her clothes in the bedroom, wondering—almost doubting, given Glenn's mood—whether Glenn would want her to sleep here tonight.

At the lake Liz plunged into the water. "Oh, I'd swim every day if I were you," she exclaimed when she broke to the surface. The water had instantly revived her.

"I do swim, sometimes," Glenn answered. Now she only dangled her feet.

Liz swam back to the dock. She put her arms on top of the boards to buoy herself. "You look exhausted."

Glenn grimaced. "I haven't been sleeping well. No, go on and swim," she said when Liz started to pull herself out of the water. "We can talk later."

Liz fell back in and swam away from shore. The water was warm on the surface, but cooler when she dove below. She played, loving the feel of the water on her. Finally Glenn jumped in.

"I couldn't resist," she said, smiling for the first time when she reached Liz. "You looked like you were having so much fun. Oh, this does feel great."

Glenn dove below and grabbed Liz at her waist. Liz felt herself being pulled under; they both burst out laughing, then choked on mouthfuls of water.

"Come on, let's swim," Glenn said. Liz followed her as she began swimming towards the middle of the lake.

"I almost feel like a new person," Glenn said after they had dried off and were back at the house. Smiling wryly, she added, "I imagine you're glad about that."

Liz walked over to her. "I liked the old one more than you think, but if you're feeling better, I am glad."

Glenn leaned forward to kiss her. Their lips brushed lightly once, then met in startling urgency. Liz moved closer, pressing against Glenn. Glenn's body felt cool and damp beneath her thin robe. Liz suddenly wanted to slip the robe off, then lower the straps of her bathing suit—

"It seems like forever since I've seen you," Glenn said softly, her eyes lingering on Liz after their kiss ended.

Liz smiled.

"Have you eaten?" Glenn asked.

Liz had. She sat down at the kitchen table and watched Glenn as she rinsed several pieces of fruit then opened packages of cheese, slicing thin strips of each onto a plate. They went out to sit on the deck.

"Glenn, are you angry with me?" Liz asked after Glenn had finished eating.

"Angry with you? No, of course not. Why would you think so?"

Liz shrugged. "I thought maybe you were. Because of Saturday night—and my being difficult." She struggled to say the words.

"Oh, Liz. I'm sorry. No. I've just been upset with myself and worried about this week's testing."

Liz wanted to look at Glenn, but she couldn't. For the better part of two days Glenn had virtually ignored her. Since Saturday night her emotions had been a roller coaster of high and low feelings—mainly low; she had been terrified to think her past had already screwed up her present. It didn't make her feel much better to think that Glenn had been more worried about work than she had been about her feelings.

"When you told me about Diana, I know it wasn't easy for you, but you did it," Liz continued, her eyes still lowered. "I don't know why it was so hard telling you about Chris."

"Liz, look at me," Glenn said, then waited until she did. "I wasn't worried about that. I want you to tell me whatever you want to tell me about yourself, when and how you want to, okay?"

Liz only nodded.

"Come on, let's go inside," Glenn said. "Right now all I want to do is hold you."

They sat together on the couch. Glenn held Liz, stroking her face and hair while Joan Armatrading sang love songs. Liz smiled when she felt Glenn leaning over, kissing her ear. She squirmed, then she giggled. "Stop it," she pleaded, laughing harder when Glenn wouldn't.

Finally Glenn did. "Pamela's coming over for dinner tomorrow night," she said. "Would you like to come over later in the evening and meet her? I have to be here all night anyway in case anyone calls from work."

"Sure. I'd like that."

"Also, Diana and Joyce have invited us for dinner on Saturday night. Would you like to go?"

"That sounds fine," Liz answered, nevertheless startled to be meeting Diana so soon.

Glenn smiled, reassuring, though Liz hadn't realized she had betrayed her anxiety.

"Sorry," Glenn said. "I know this seems like a lot all at once. But Diana and Joyce wanted to have a dinner party. And Pamela—well, I see Pamela often. Don't worry, I think you'll enjoy them."

❋

"Do you mean to tell me Liz doesn't know about California yet?" Pamela asked as Glenn refilled the two cups on the coffee table. Glenn had just admitted as much.

"Things have been happening faster than I expected between us," Glenn said. "I'm sorry now for not having said anything. Before, it didn't seem necessary. This was supposed to be a safe situation, remember?"

"Yes. You kind of like her, don't you?"

"Yes, I do like her, kind of," Glenn replied, teasing Pam.

"What *is* happening with the job in California?"

Glenn took a sip of coffee, hiding her frown. "Actually, the woman at the consulting firm called me this week. She's working on a different position than the one she and I talked about in June." Glenn didn't add that she had felt more tempted by Ann Carlyle's description of the new job than she had wanted to be. "Honestly, there are times when I'm sorry I started all of this," she ended.

"All of what?" Pamela demanded sharply.

"Job searching."

Liz arrived shortly afterwards. When Glenn went to open the door, Pamela moved to the chair at the end of the coffee table, leaving room for Liz on the sofa.

"I understand some rather important things are going on at work these days," Pamela said to Liz after Glenn had introduced them.

"Well, yes. I guess you could say that," Liz replied, sounding stiff though Glenn recognized light irony in her voice.

"So what do you think? Is the new system going to work?"

Glenn laughed to see Liz subjected so quickly to Pam's rapid-fire questions. She had failed to warn Liz about that.

"*I* think it's going to work," Liz said, clearly exaggerating. "Not everyone shares that opinion, however."

"I'll wait until tomorrow before offering my own opinion, thank you just the same," Glenn said, reaching over and shaking Liz playfully. "I just don't know where these upstart students get their ideas," she said to Pamela. "The first day on the job and they start telling everyone what to do!"

"As I recall, that was not exactly how my first day started," Liz said. "Let me think, what did you say to me—"

Pamela burst out laughing. "Tell me the story," she pleaded, ignoring Glenn's objections.

Glenn suffered through Liz's version, interrupting vehemently when she felt too much maligned. Already she sensed Liz and Pam liked each other. And why shouldn't they, she asked herself silently—they're both funny and warm and wonderful.

Pamela was laughing so hard she had to wipe tears from her eyes. Glenn smiled at her, then looked closer, seeing more

131

than tears of laughter. There was unmistakable happiness in Pamela's eyes—a happiness she hadn't seen in Pam in a long time. Glenn frowned, knowing what Pam was thinking—that now that she had met Liz there was no way she would move to California.

Glenn thought again of the phone call she had had the other night. One more week, Ann Carlyle had promised, ten days at the most. She was nearly ready to make a firm offer.

Glenn reminded herself she had heard promises from this woman before.

———

The old method of the quarterly closing had apparently run without difficulty. Glenn awoke the next morning, at once relieved and anxious. No one had called with word of a problem. Today, then, would be the day for the real test. Could their new system outperform the old?

Throughout the morning she, Laura and Liz worked to check the closing's results. It was a tedious process, but the numbers matched what they had expected. Glenn went to lunch, then to a brief meeting with Bob and one of the plant managers. She wasn't able to submit the new process until two o'clock.

For the next hour she paced through the department, belatedly realizing she was disrupting her entire staff, but by three-thirty she had the new reports on her desk. Glenn stared in disbelief at the pages—the new process had executed four times faster than the old one! Laura and Liz came in to help her compare results.

By five-thirty Glenn knew the runs had produced identical reports. Her excitement swelled as they reached the final page—it had worked. It was incredible: a simple trick and Liz had fooled the computer into thinking it had more space for holding their data than it did. Glenn sat back in her chair and looked at Liz, once again filled with admiration for her talent.

"Well," Liz said anxiously, "are you convinced now?"

"You'd better believe it," Glenn said. "Let's celebrate. I'm buying."

The three women went to a bar where they had gone once before. Liz and Glenn stayed behind after Laura left. For the first time Glenn asked Liz where she had come up with this idea and why, given everything, she had taken the trouble to develop it.

"I might have had the idea," Liz said when she finished, "but you're the one who made it work. This project is your success, Glenn, not mine."

Glenn laughed and looked away. "No, it's yours and Laura's. I still can't believe how hard you both worked."

"Glenn, you were the one who gave us something to work on. You did a great job of thinking through all of the details that had to be changed. It worked the first time because you didn't miss a thing."

Glenn smiled but continued to gaze distractedly across the room. "So much has happened so fast. I can't believe this is all over."

"It was my understanding this was just the beginning— no less than the dawn of a new era in Materials/Finance."

Glenn shook her head and said only, "Right."

———

Completely exhausted, Glenn spent Friday night and most of Saturday alone. Liz came over late Saturday afternoon. That evening they went to Diana's.

"I have to say, I'm feeling a little nervous about this dinner," Liz confessed as they got into Glenn's car.

"Don't be," Glenn said. "Diana and Joyce are both great talkers. You already know that Pamela is. You probably won't get in a word all night."

At the front door of the house, Glenn leaned over and whispered to Liz, "You look wonderful."

Liz looked startled, but grateful, as Diana opened the front door.

Glenn almost had to laugh at how warmly Diana and Joyce greeted Liz. Graciousness all but oozed from Diana. She was dressed simply tonight, wearing blue jeans and a pale yellow polo shirt. And Joyce—with her round, wire-rimmed glasses sliding halfway down her nose and her wisps of curly dark hair always escaping the clip at the back of her neck— Glenn thought she looked more like a Shakespearean scholar than the vice president of marketing which she was.

"Something smells wonderful," Glenn exclaimed.

Diana came around the others and brushed her lips lightly against Glenn's cheek. "Joyce has worked her usual magic in the kitchen. Come on in."

Glenn put her arm around Liz as they walked through the house to the back. Sitting outside, Diana at once began telling an outrageously funny story; before she finished, she

133

had drawn Liz into the conversation, seemingly innocently and effortlessly. Glenn smiled faintly—Diana had remembered her promise to behave well. Glenn was impressed at how quickly she had made Liz feel at ease.

Pamela arrived soon afterwards. Without Cynthia. It was over, she announced to the others, then followed that with the equally startling news that she was never going to fall in love again.

Everyone laughed, ignoring Pamela's insistent objections that this time she meant what she said.

Still tired, but now relaxed, Glenn felt a quiet happiness in being with her friends and with Liz. If only it were always this simple, she thought silently at one point. It could be; if she chose it, it could be. She looked up and saw Diana's bright smile, at that moment meant for Liz. Who could resist her, Glenn thought; nobody could, and certainly not Liz just now. Glenn smiled to herself and wondered how she had ever survived losing Diana. But she hadn't lost her. Diana was somehow, through Liz, making it clear how much she still loved her.

Joyce broke into the conversation. Glenn turned to watch her. Joyce—the only person Glenn had ever known who could ignore Diana in her moments of rage. Good thing, she thought—and thought also how much she had grown to love Joyce in this last year.

And Pamela. Glenn's eyes fell as she glanced to her left to look at Pamela. The trust and the love they shared, had nurtured through so many years of friendship—no one would ever take Pamela's place in her life.

Glenn's eyes moved more slowly to her right, resting on Liz's flushed face. Liz was saying something to Joyce, Glenn didn't know what. The unexpected continued to be just that: Liz's presence in her life defied all things rational. For many reasons. But there she was, answering a question, causing Joyce to laugh. Glenn smiled too, as if she were in on the joke. How long would it last—how long could it last? Weren't all relationships wonderful in the beginning?

Most frustrating of all, why did she have to answer these questions so quickly? Maybe she didn't. Maybe there never would be a job in San Francisco about which she had to decide.

Glenn had no idea how much time had passed. She was surprised, when she looked up, to have her eyes lock on

Diana's: Diana, apparently, had watched her watch the others. Immediately Diana looked away, almost guiltily. In the next moment she looked back, her eyes quiet and serious. Then her somberness was broken by a guileless smile. For Diana it was a rare expression. Glenn met her gaze and smiled, too. It was as though in that moment they exchanged an unspoken acknowledgement of something, something that between them perhaps always would be unspoken—a bond, or a love, or a commitment.

Glenn's gaze fell down to the table, to the empty plates all around. Her thoughts fell silent. This was her life; these women were her friends. A moment later she looked up and rejoined the conversation.

❋

Ann Carlyle called on Monday night.

"I have great news for you, Glenn. The position I spoke to you about last week opened today. The job is yours if you want it." She went on to describe in greater detail a high-profile position in a fast-growing company in which Glenn would be overseeing the development of a new financial system.

"Think about it, Glenn, but don't wait too long," she ended. "We'll be glad to fly you out here if you'd like to talk to the owner of the company. Sheila Ryan would like to meet you."

Glenn hung up the phone in a blaze of frustration, silently cursing everything she could think to name. The offer tempted her. She hadn't wanted to be tempted, but she was. She had her offer—now all she had to do was make her decision.

———

Thursday was Liz's last day. The entire department, including Glenn, went out to lunch. At the restaurant, Liz and Laura sat next to each other at one end of the table. Glenn sat away from them, at the other end. She chatted idly with Donna and the others who sat near her, but she felt her eyes drawn often to Liz.

After lunch Liz sat in Glenn's office facing her for one last time.

"It's hard to believe this is it," Liz said.

Glenn smiled. "Where are you going with Alice tonight?"

"I don't know yet. Did you want to get together later?"

"No," Glenn answered quickly, knowing she had a busy night ahead, even if it was only to do more of the same fruitless thinking she had been doing all week. "Just have fun with Alice tonight. We'll be together all weekend."

Liz left soon afterwards. Later in the afternoon Glenn glanced up to see Laura at her door.

"Already it seems too quiet around here, doesn't it?" Laura asked, referring to Liz's absence.

Glenn smiled and agreed.

"Liz said Bob offered her a job here, anytime she wants to come back."

"I know. Speaking of jobs," Glenn continued, her tone more serious, "there's something I've wanted to ask you for a while, Laura. What are your plans—your career plans? I don't want to put you on the spot, so just say so if you'd rather not talk about this."

Laura did seem taken aback, but she said, "I don't mind talking." She laughed shortly. "I like working for you, Glenn. I won't pretend I haven't thought about looking for a different job—something more in project management. On the other hand, I don't know if I'm that ambitious." She looked curiously at Glenn when she stopped.

"How would you feel about staying on in this department if I left?" Glenn asked. Bob, of course, would choose her successor, but Glenn had always assumed Laura would move up when she left.

Laura looked shocked. "I don't know," she said, stumbling. "I really don't. Are you leaving, Glenn?"

Glenn shrugged. "I've thought about it. With everything that's happened this summer, I think things can get better around here. But I don't know."

"Do you have another offer?" Laura asked, surprising Glenn with the directness of her question.

"Yes, I do," Glenn answered, though she had intended not to reveal this. "Please don't say anything to anyone, Laura. I really haven't made up my mind what I want to do."

———

When she got home that night Glenn reread the confirmation letter Ann Carlyle had sent her. Nothing had changed—not the words on the page, not her own confusion about what to do.

The problem with the job was that it sounded wonderful. Last night she had been certain she wanted to make another trip west, at least to talk about this new position. Now, she wasn't sure. What was the point—was there a point?

The point at the moment was that if she took this job she'd be working for a woman. For years she had wanted the chance to work for a woman. Glenn rubbed her temples wearily and reminded herself that she didn't even know this woman—Sheila Ryan. She had absolutely no reason to believe working for her would be any better than working for Bob.

Glenn stood up and walked outside to the deck. She stood at the edge, gripping the thin railing with both hands. The lake blended black into the black of night, but she felt it rippling gently near.

The house that Diana built, she thought, running her fingers over the smooth wood, overcome suddenly by the memory of the life she had lived here with Diana.

Because, after all, wasn't the point still Diana?

For more than a year Glenn knew she had pretended otherwise, but deep in her heart she had never believed she would get over Diana—not until she put real time and space between them. Moving to California was supposed to accomplish that.

And maybe it would, and maybe it wouldn't, she thought, sighing as she turned from the railing to sit in a chair. Now she had met Liz and all of her questions seemed so much harder.

The questions haunted her through the night and through the next day. She spent the day—Friday—home alone.

Late in the afternoon Glenn made her decision. She called Ann Carlyle to tell her.

❦

On Friday night Liz and Glenn left for Vermont. Rain had fallen throughout the day, though now it was not much more than a steady drizzle. It promised to be a long, wet drive.

Liz, driving, thought Glenn seemed especially quiet. Glenn had said she'd not worked that day, but she hadn't explained how she had spent her time. Liz had to fight back feelings of jealousy that Glenn had taken a day off and had shown no sign of wanting to spend the time with her.

Late that night they reached southern Vermont and found the cottage they had reserved for the weekend. Liz smiled to herself, noting its waterfront location: in many ways

137

it resembled Glenn's house. Still, it was good to get away from home, away from ordinary routines and distractions.

Glenn collapsed on the bed while Liz made one last trip to the car. She returned and shut and locked the cabin door then removed her damp jacket. In the bedroom Glenn extended one arm to her. Liz walked over and sat down.

"This weekend, you and I are going to have to do some talking," Glenn said.

Liz smiled and said, "I know." She had an agenda of her own, but it eased her mind to know Glenn also felt the need to talk.

The next morning they slept in late. When they got up they drove into a nearby town to have breakfast.

Liz knew she had to talk to Glenn. For days she had been thinking about what to say. During the periods of silence at breakfast she debated when to share her thoughts. She decided to wait until they were back at the cottage.

It was the middle of the afternoon before they returned. Inside, Liz sat in an overstuffed chair which appeared to be more comfortable than it actually was. Glenn sat near her in a matching chair. Liz alternated between resting her feet on the coffee table in front of her as Glenn did and pulling her legs beneath her to sit cross-legged. Feeling nervous, she changed her position often.

"Glenn, I've been thinking I need to talk to you about some things," she said, starting in a spontaneous burst.

Glenn looked up. "What is it?" she asked.

Instantly Liz regretted having started. She shifted her position, tucking her feet beneath her and leaning forward. Reluctant now, she said, "I know we haven't been seeing each other for very long, but there are some things I need to tell you."

Glenn smiled and said, "Okay."

"Well, I just want you to know that our relationship is very important to me. I want to do whatever I can to make it stronger. I know that the most important thing in any relationship is for two people to be able to talk to each other." She paused to smile. "I also know that I'm not always good about being open. But I want to tell you that I will always try to be honest with you. I will tell you whatever you want to know about me, and I will always try very hard to share my feelings with you."

Glenn's smile softened.

Liz hadn't finished. "One of the things that I have to tell you is that I think I've been intimidated by you. I don't know if that's because of the working relationship we've had or if I've just been frightened of you. I do know that I've tended to hold back and wait to follow your lead. I know that's not a good thing. So, I have to stop myself from doing that."

Liz stopped. She struggled to frame the words she still wanted to say.

"Maybe I wanted you to feel that way," Glenn said softly, interrupting before she could continue.

Liz looked up in surprise.

"Liz, I also need to talk to you. There have been some things going on in my life which I haven't told you about. Several months ago I interviewed for a job in San Francisco. Had I been offered the job then, I would have accepted it and moved. We never would have gotten involved. The offer was delayed. At that time, I was told that it would be about six weeks before they could make any offer. It took even longer than that, but this past week I was offered the job. I spent yesterday trying to decide what I wanted to do." Glenn stopped. "I turned the job down," she ended.

Liz was stunned. She stared at Glenn, confused and unable to respond.

"Until yesterday I didn't know what I was going to do," Glenn continued. "Before, I think I kept hoping I wouldn't have to make a decision. I do know that I've tried to hold myself back, both from you and from admitting to myself what I feel for you, because of this. I suppose I have wanted to control this relationship—or at least how willing I've been to get involved with you."

Liz felt overwhelmed. "Why didn't you tell me?" she asked when Glenn stopped.

Glenn shrugged. "I don't know. I didn't expect to get this involved with you. Maybe I was just being selfish in trying to keep you out, insisting on my right to decide the course of my own life apart from your or anyone else's influence."

Hearing this, Liz stood up and walked to the window. A hard knot was in her stomach; intense anguish gripped the muscles in her throat. Staring but not seeing anything through the panes of smudged glass, she struggled to understand what Glenn had said.

A minute passed. She turned to Glenn. "What was this to you—an affair?"

Glenn grimaced. "It was. In the beginning."

"Well, it never was to me!" Liz whirled around to face the window.

Glenn walked over and stood near her. "What is this to you, Liz?"

Liz answered by taking a step towards the door.

"No. Don't leave."

Liz stopped and glanced backwards. "I have to. I'm too confused."

"Liz, you just said you want to be able to tell me what you're thinking and feeling. Please, tell me now."

"I can't. The idea of your moving," Liz said, still shocked by Glenn's admission. "I don't know, maybe you didn't owe me any explanation. I can't help it. I'm upset." She started for the door.

"So, what you said earlier was all conditional then?" Glenn asked, her tone accusing. "You can tell me what's going on inside as long as it's easy? Liz, I made my decision to stay here because I want this relationship with you. Can't you at least stay and talk about it?"

Liz flinched when she heard these words. Uncertainly, she looked at Glenn.

"Liz," Glenn said, stepping forward.

Liz turned away quickly, feeling tears spring to her eyes, unwilling for Glenn to see them.

Outside the window a windsurfer fell as she watched. The body splashed into the water; a moment later the person's head reappeared. It's funny the things you notice, Liz thought. Everything inside herself seemed to be steadily dissolving; she didn't try to clutch, to hold all or any part of it together. Instead, she watched the irrelevant actions of the distant individual, unknown, and unknowing, a part of her life here.

"I'm in love with you, Glenn. I've been in love with you for a long time." Liz trembled as she spoke. She had never felt more frightened to speak the truth.

"Are you really?" Glenn came closer and placed her hands on her shoulders.

"Yes."

"It's a funny thing. I'm in love with you, too."

Liz turned and hugged Glenn tightly, unconcerned now by her tears falling freely. Glenn struggled to speak through her own broken sobs.

"Liz, I have been so miserable this past year," Glenn said after they had moved to sit on the sofa. "I would have done anything to change my life. When I met you, then started seeing you, I had no idea that our relationship would be different from any of the other relationships I've gotten into and out of in the last year."

As though a dam had burst, her words poured out.

"I've felt so angry with everyone. I've pretended to be happy, but my life has been nothing more than repeating a familiar set of motions, doing and saying what people around me expect, never getting any satisfaction in return. I couldn't take it any more. That's when I decided to move to California."

Glenn stopped to take a deep breath. "I felt so self-righteous every time I thought about moving. It was my way of saying 'This is my life, and I can live it as I please!' I didn't want anyone telling me what I should or shouldn't do—not Diana, not Pamela, and then not you. Once I talked myself into moving it was ten times harder to talk myself out of it, even though everything inside of me was telling me not to go. I'm sorry I never told you about this. I'm sorry that I haven't told you all of the things that I've thought and felt since we've been involved. I've been so afraid that you would be angry. Are you?"

"No," Liz answered, meaning it sincerely.

The sofa was as uncomfortable as the chairs it matched. Liz and Glenn went into the bedroom, to their bed.

"I am so frightened of what I feel for you," Glenn said when they were lying down. "This whole last year I was sure all I wanted was to be involved in a good, stable relationship. Now I feel terrified of that. I'm afraid to trust myself, and I'm afraid to trust you. But I love you, I know I do. And I know how happy I feel when I'm with you."

Glenn was quiet after that. All Liz wanted was to hold her, to console her somehow for the sorrow of the last year. The strain of the last weeks—the strain in Glenn over the entire summer—Liz thought she understood everything now so much better.

"Liz," Glenn said softly, breaking their brief silence, "what does all of this mean to you?"

Liz was frightened by the directness of her question.

"Let me start over," Glenn said. "How do you really feel about being involved with me?"

141

Liz hesitated a second time. Then she replied, "I love you, Glenn. I meant it when I said I want our relationship to be strong. I'll do anything."

"I don't want to know what you'll do, Liz. I want to know how you feel."

Liz saw the smile on Glenn's face, but it didn't ease her fear. "How do I feel?" She laughed and stared straight up at the ceiling. "I feel like life is worth living. I want to run and scream and jump and shout and tell all the world I love you. I love you, Glenn. I never want to stop saying that." Tears were in her eyes. "Everything has been so hard for so long. Now it doesn't matter. I feel free. I only have to look at you to feel happy. Sometimes I feel like I never want to take my eyes away from you. I guess I'm afraid you'll disappear. Or maybe that my feelings will." She said the last softly. Large tears rolled down her face.

"Come here," Glenn said. Liz moved closer into her arms. "Nobody gets any guarantees," Glenn said.

No guarantees, Liz thought. Then what was their promise for the future?

There had to be some promise. For the feelings they shared, for the love they had for each other—there had to be some way to say, *this is forever*. Liz cried because she knew there wasn't.

"Can you tell me why you're crying?" Glenn asked.

"Because I want to know this feeling will last."

"Oh Liz, there are so many ways to love. We have this way now. Some other day it will be different, but it will be our love."

"I guess you think I'm silly," Liz said embarrassed by her tears.

"No. I think you're beautiful." Glenn leaned over to kiss her. "And right now there's only one thing in the world I want to do—"

Liz looked at her.

"I want to make love with you."

Chapter Eleven

It was a Saturday in mid-September. Liz went to the windows at the balcony of Glenn's room. In one carefully considered move, she pulled the cord, opening wide and without warning the thick drapes.

Glenn, still in bed, complained loudly; she reached for Liz's pillow and covered her head. Liz walked back to the bed and tried to think what to do next. She pulled the sheet away from Glenn. Glenn, blinded by the pillow still over her eyes, reached wildly for the sheet. Liz by then was sitting next to her, leaning over her, kissing her ribs.

"Have I told you lately that I'm crazy about your body?" Liz said, moving her mouth slowly to Glenn's breast.

Glenn stopped protesting. "Umm," she said instead. "No, I don't think you have mentioned that. Tell me more." She pushed the pillow away and looked up.

"Good. You're awake. We can go now."

Glenn's eyebrows knitted into a pout. "Why can't we just stay here?"

Liz replied by offering her hand. "Come on. The sooner I get done at school, the more time we'll have to be together later."

"What would you like to do later today?" Glenn asked while they waited for their breakfast at a diner in Watertown. "I have a couple of ideas. We could play tourists at Quincy Market. Or, we could try to look suave and sophisticated and go to the shops in Back Bay. Or, we could just be lazy and pick up sandwiches and sit by the river."

"I don't care. You decide," Liz said, just then catching herself mooning across the table at Glenn. "No, I know. Let's go to Back Bay. We can walk to Northeastern and you can tell me stories about your wild college days."

After breakfast, they stopped at the apartment. Alice squinted up from the kitchen table when they entered. Staring at Liz, she stroked her cheek thoughtfully and muttered, quite plainly, "Your face is familiar, but I can't remember where we met."

Liz scowled, feigning annoyance. "It's nice to see you, too. I wondered whether you had moved, but your mail kept coming here."

"Now I remember you," Alice called out after Liz had turned to go to her room. "I think I saw you the other morning—that was you in my bathroom, wasn't it?"

Glenn and Alice were talking when Liz returned to the kitchen, having gathered the clothes she needed for the rest of the weekend.

"So, going to school today?" Alice said, raising one eyebrow. "A hot date at BU—I'll tell you, Edwards, you really know how to show a girl a good time."

Liz frowned, more annoyed now. "I only need to work for an hour. You wouldn't believe how crowded the computer center already is," she added.

"Better get used to it," Alice said knowingly to Glenn. "Once school started last year, I only saw her, oh, maybe three or four times between September and May. Not that I didn't get my fill of her when I did see her. It doesn't look like I'll have to worry about her company wearing thin at all this year."

Glenn laughed, but Liz was irritated. Alice's message couldn't be any clearer: she was angry with her. But as many nights as Alice spent away from the apartment, Liz didn't think she had much right to complain that she herself was there so infrequently now.

"Don't forget about soccer on Tuesday night," Alice said as Liz and Glenn headed for the door. "It's just a pickup game. But I suppose these days you don't need to do any picking up."

"Sorry about that," Liz said to Glenn as they descended the outside steps. "Alice must have been turned down last night. I don't know why she was so bitchy."

144

Glenn put her arm around Liz and shook her playfully. "Oh, you worry too much. I thought she was funny."

———

Late in the afternoon in the middle of the next week Liz managed to finish her day early. Although it was still only the beginning of the semester, already she felt wary of the volume of work her courses would require. Thrilled to have even one evening with no tasks outstanding, she left school to drive to Glenn's.

The temperature had soared that day; by late afternoon it was still quite warm. A light breeze stirred the mild air. Driving away from the city, her car windows rolled down, Liz thought this one of her favorite kinds of days.

When she reached the house the front door was wide open. Liz walked in and saw Glenn talking on the phone. Something in the way Glenn nervously kicked the coffee table, and hearing her voice, unfamiliarly strained, worried Liz. She had no idea to whom Glenn was speaking.

The conversation ended almost immediately. Glenn replaced the receiver, said hello, but remained downcast.

"What's up?" Liz asked.

"That was my mother. The cold war continues."

Liz didn't know much about Glenn's family—only that her parents had been upset when she came out to them. Glenn had said their relationship, especially her and her mother's, had changed since then.

"I don't even know why I care any more!" Glenn said. "My parents make me so angry. Maybe I won't bother going home this Christmas."

"That seems a little extreme," Liz said softly. "Isn't Christmas the only time you see them now?"

Glenn shrugged. In the same angry voice, she said, "Why does she have to be so unreasonable? Why can't she accept me for who I am?"

"Let's go down by the water," Liz suggested. "It's such a nice day. We can talk there."

They went to the dock and sat down on the boards, still warm from the hot day's sun. A mild breeze blew in from the water. Children in a rowboat were chasing a few of the lake's remaining ducks and geese.

"One of these days I think I'm going to have to shoot my parents," Glenn declared.

Liz laughed, not shocked at the violence in her words.

"Seriously—I'm thirty-one years old now. Don't I have the right to be out from under their influence?"

Looking at Glenn, Liz saw for the first time not the mature woman who was her lover, but a rebellious child still dueling for independence. "Why do you think they still have so much influence over you? I would have thought that with everything that's happened, that would have changed."

Glenn's frown deepened. "Me too. No such luck. Sometimes, when I think about my parents, I feel as if a fist is tightly clenched inside of me, squeezing harder. There's always something I have to do or be to stay in their good graces. Being myself is never good enough."

"Things changed after you came out to them, right?" Liz prompted when Glenn did not go on.

Glenn sighed angrily. "Yes. That's when things changed."

"What happened when you told them?"

Glenn didn't answer right away. She was leaning backwards, braced against her hands. As she looked out over the lake the breeze caught the curl on her forehead and lifted it, trying, with each gust, to sweep it back. Liz couldn't see Glenn's eyes, but she knew they gazed, unfocused, at the water.

"My first mistake was assuming they already knew what was going on. They didn't. Diana and I had just decided to live together and I felt like I was on top of the world. I don't know, maybe some of Diana's arrogance or feelings of omnipotence rubbed off on me and I thought I could get away with anything. I just blurted it out during one visit and was totally unprepared for their reaction. I didn't want anything to ruin the excitement I felt over Diana, so I responded to their outrage with my own outrage. We all said things I'm sure we regret—my mother, my father, myself. In the space of one evening it seemed my relationship with them disintegrated. I was foolish enough to think that losing them didn't matter, that I had spent enough years trying to win an approval that they certainly wouldn't give to me now. It seemed that the game was finally over, and in an unexpected way, I was making my escape."

Glenn stopped and stared down at the dock.

Softly, she continued, "More than anything I miss talking to my mother. She could see through me better than anyone. Just like you." Glenn almost smiled as she looked at Liz.

"When Diana and I broke up I couldn't even tell her. She and my father probably would have thought that justice had been served, to lose Diana after the way I threw her at them. One day, months after Diana left, my mother accidentally asked about her, so I told her then. Do you know how much that hurt? All I wanted was to fall apart and tell her how terrible I felt and listen to her tell me that everything would be all right. But I couldn't do that. We'll probably never have that kind of relationship again."

"You don't know," Liz said. "People change. Situations change. I'm sure your parents still love you very much. You just threw them a real curve and they're not over it."

"That was four years ago! If they're not over it by now, what makes you think they ever will be?"

"I don't know," Liz admitted. More pensively, she continued, "This might sound funny, but in a way, I envy you. I've never felt very close to either of my parents. At least you and your parents had a good relationship once, even though it's not so great at the moment."

Glenn smirked. "Isn't there a line in some song—when you have more, you have more to lose—?"

"That's not what I meant. I was just thinking that, since you did have a good relationship, maybe this is something you can still work through."

"I'm not convinced they'll try any more."

"Your not going home at Christmas would amount to the same thing."

Glenn laughed. "So, Ms. Know-it-all, any suggestions?"

"No," Liz conceded.

The light had dimmed considerably while they talked. An eerie orange glow showed in the western sky where a short time ago the sun had set. Voices from the children in the rowboat, now heading towards shore, carried across the water. Glenn lay down on the dock; she placed her hands behind her head and watched the slow-passing clouds. Tears swelled in her eyes but did not fall. She held them there, losing thought and memory as she followed the path of one cloud as it drifted away. Afterwards, she blinked her tears back and turned to look at Liz. Liz was sitting with her chin on her knee, staring at the water, deep in thought over something. Glenn smiled; there was no telling what Liz was thinking. A sharp spasm shook her and she felt how much she loved Liz.

147

It wasn't just the way her body opened to Liz when they made love, Glenn thought, gazing again at the clouds, wondering what drew her so strongly to Liz. Nor was it her intelligence, or her easy sense of humor, though she loved her for both. It certainly wasn't that she was an athlete, or that she had such passion for playing soccer. Or such passion for her classes.

Glenn felt her eyes filling with tears again. She sat up and kissed Liz's shoulder. Liz turned around and smiled, then her eyes softened in concern when she saw her tears. Glenn brushed her eyes. "It's okay," she said. She tried to laugh. "We finally get a night together—I don't want to ruin it by being upset."

Liz moved closer and put one arm around her. Glenn leaned her head on Liz's shoulder. "I wish you could be here every night, Liz," she said. "I miss you when we're not together. I just miss you."

Liz held her tighter. "I'm here now," she said.

Glenn nodded. "I know. I'm just feeling greedy."

❁

Glenn leaned all the way across Liz and reached for the framed photo on the nightstand. Holding the picture of Jennette and Louise above her, she said, "This might sound silly, but sometimes I feel more jealous of Jennette than I do of anyone else in your life, including any of your ex-lovers."

Liz looked at the picture in Glenn's hands. "That is silly," she agreed.

Glenn continued, "I don't mean jealous like I'm afraid you want to run off with her. I mean jealous of how you feel about her. Whenever Jennette's name comes up, right away I feel all of this feeling you have for her. Sometimes it's hard for me to tell how you really feel about other people or other things. With Jennette, I always know."

Glenn studied the photo of the two women a moment longer: Jennette, Liz's first friend in Boston, bundled up on a cold, windy day at the coast, but smiling, clearly happy— Glenn could practically feel the love in Jennette through this lifeless picture; Jennette's arm around Louise, her lover, whose teaching job had taken them both to Philadelphia. After reaching across Liz a second time to set the photo down, Glenn rolled slowly back to her own side of the bed, enjoying the brief moment when her body was pressed against Liz. "I always assumed you thought of Alice as your best friend," she said. "But when I hear you talk about Jennette, it's like you feel closest to her."

"I feel close to them both. Actually, things with Alice aren't so great at the moment," Liz admitted.

"Why? Did something happen?"

"Not that I know of, except when she was in such a snit that morning we stopped here. I think Alice is mad at me. For not being around much, I guess."

"I thought you told me she's not here much when she's seeing someone—or not here alone, anyway."

"She's not. So I don't know why my not being here is different."

"Are you going to talk to her?"

"I hadn't planned to. It's just been a bad coincidence that we've been here on the same nights so infrequently."

Glenn smiled to herself; she would have been completely shocked had Liz said she intended to do anything but wait and see if things with Alice didn't work out without any intervention. Yet at the same time she felt a twinge of regret at this casual reminder of how unwilling Liz so often was to talk about her feelings.

Glenn rolled on to her side and began running her fingers across Liz's forehead and through her hair. "So, will I ever get to meet Jennette?" she asked, returning to their original conversation.

"Oh sure. She and Louise come to Boston often. In her last letter, Jennette said they're hoping to get back to Boston for a visit this fall. I haven't seen them since last March, when I visited them in Philadelphia."

Irrationally, Glenn felt stung by the energy she heard in Liz's voice. Then suddenly she felt disturbed to realize Liz's affection was for someone who lived hundreds of miles away. Did Liz find it so easy to express her feelings for Jennette only because she was so distant?

"Liz, can we talk about something," Glenn started, disliking the tentativeness she heard in her own voice.

"Sure. What?"

"Living together."

Liz neither responded nor altered her expression, but Glenn felt a subtle shift of tension between them.

"Don't you think it might simplify our lives if we lived together?" Glenn continued anyway.

"Simplify things? No. I think it would complicate them. At least initially."

"Liz, just listen to me for a second, okay? You know I've been upset about how little time we have together. Part of what I get upset about is not knowing when I'm going to be able to see you. If we were living together, then I'd know I'd see you every night. I know the drive to school from my house would be harder for you. But I think things would be better in a lot of other ways."

"Glenn, doesn't it seem too soon to be talking about living together?" Liz pleaded. "We've only been seeing each other for two months."

Glenn looked at her. "I know I want to live with you. I've told you that."

"And I want to live with you. But I don't think this is the right time to make that decision."

"Why not?"

Liz only shrugged unhappily.

"Besides," Glenn went on, resuming stroking Liz's forehead, "if you moved out of here, you wouldn't have to pay rent."

"I'd have to pay you."

"Why? I know you've been worried about money. I've been paying that mortgage by myself for the last year. Think how much you'd save."

"You've got this all figured out, haven't you?" Liz said, a first note of anger in her voice.

Glenn searched Liz's eyes, looking for anything to soften what she heard in her words.

———

"You look tired," Pamela said to Glenn at dinner in Harvard Square that night. Liz had just gone to the bathroom. Julie, an old friend of Pam's visiting for the weekend, had promptly left the table to follow her.

"I am, a little," Glenn answered.

"Working too hard?"

"No. Not any harder than usual." Glenn smiled wanly. "Lately I've been discovering how little tolerance I have for Liz's schedule. Don't ever get involved with a student," she said heatedly, then added, "Sorry. I don't mean that. I'm not being a very good sport. Silly me, I want romance all the time."

Pamela smiled. "You always do. But everything else is okay?"

Glenn nodded. Everything except having to put up with Julie again, she thought but didn't say.

Outside the restaurant, Glenn and Liz said goodbye, declining, for the last time, Julie's invitation to go on to the bar. Reaching the narrow side street where they had parked, they decided to continue walking.

It was a cool night in early autumn. Harvard Square was jammed, as usual. Liz and Glenn stood with a crowd near the Coop, listening to four street musicians. Then they left the congestion of the university area and walked towards the river.

At the bike path they turned to walk along the river. The lights of the city blazed brightly in front of them. Glenn put her arm around Liz while they walked.

"Did you enjoy yourself tonight?" Glenn asked.

"I did. And you?"

"Yes. Although I can't say that Julie is one of my favorite people in the world."

"I thought she was nice. This was the first time I've ever been around any of your friends who knew anything about soccer."

"Julie's not really a friend," Glenn said quickly.

Near the boathouse, Glenn led Liz from the path to where trees and shrubs shielded them from the view of the few others out walking. In the shadows of one tree, Glenn leaned towards Liz, kissing her tenderly at first, then more passionately. Liz murmured softly, pulling Glenn closer when she started to move away. Then Glenn did move back, but her eyes continued to hold Liz, Liz's face, her eyes barely visible in the scant light.

"If you don't have any plans for the rest of the evening," Glenn said, smiling as she reached for Liz's hand, "I have a few ideas of my own."

Back at the apartment, a candle on the chest of drawers flickered dimly, the room's only light. Meg and Chris were singing; Liz had put on the tape from Carnegie Hall, the long tape.

Glenn slid her hand across Liz when they were naked beneath the covers. Liz's eyes stayed on her as Glenn moved her hand, tracing lines and circles over Liz's stomach, then higher, moving to her breast, rubbing her nipple. Glenn smiled when she heard Liz's breath, suddenly drawn sharper.

Glenn moved to lie on top of Liz; she lowered her mouth until their lips touched, their mouths opening into each other. Glenn pushed her tongue into Liz in long, even thrusts. Then she withdrew it—smiling to herself to feel Liz raising her head, her eyes closed now but her mouth still seeking Glenn's.

The wanting, Glenn loved to feel Liz wanting her.

Liz opened her eyes. "You're teasing me," she said.

Glenn nodded.

Liz pulled Glenn's head towards hers until their mouths met. It was Liz's tongue now, twisting around hers. Glenn felt Liz stroking both sides of her body, her fingers teasing lightly along her side, at her breasts. But the small cries Glenn heard now were her own.

Then Glenn sat up, pushing the sheet away. It was cool without it, but she needed to see Liz. She sat over her at her hips, staring at her pale skin and dark hair, the long strands in stark contrast against the white of the pillow. Liz reached up and began running her fingers along Glenn's chest, brushing across her breasts. Slowly, she drew lower until her fingers touched Glenn's dark hair.

Glenn slid lower, then leaned over and began kissing Liz below her breast. Her tongue traced over her, along her ribs, into her soft belly, wet circles at her flat hips. Liz moaned softly, knowing how Glenn was going to touch her. Then Glenn kissed her harder, moving into her legs, using her hands now, hesitating with her tongue, then pressing the tip of her tongue so lightly, barely there, into Liz. Glenn felt Liz's body moving underneath her; she heard her cries, all pleasure.

Glenn slid her fingers into Liz. Liz opened to her, welcoming every touch. Glenn pressed deeper. Then she stopped, hardly touching her, her tongue still on her but not moving. Seconds passed while Glenn waited for Liz's hunger to grow—for Liz to feel more, to feel everything when she touched her again.

Liz's hips rocked softly, trying to persuade her. Still Glenn waited.

Then, not waiting, Glenn pressed her tongue against Liz. Liz groaned, lost in new pleasure. Denying her nothing, Glenn poured the rhythm of her touch deep into Liz until she heard her loud cry and felt her release.

When Liz was quiet, Glenn moved to lie alongside her. She pulled Liz into her arms, loving her, cradling her in her arms and in her love, waiting, but not impatient for Liz to make love to her.

Chapter Twelve

Alice was stretched out on the recliner when Liz returned to the apartment.

"What a long day—I'm exhausted," Liz said.

Alice sat up. "Glenn called," she said somberly. "Four times. You were supposed to be at her house for dinner."

"Oh my god," Liz gasped. "Diana and Joyce."

Alice nodded.

Liz sank onto the couch. Her stomach was instantly churning.

"I didn't know how to get in touch with you," Alice said, almost as though to apologize.

Liz stood up and put on the jacket she had just removed. She headed for the front door.

"Aren't you going to call Glenn?" Alice called.

"No. I just have to go there."

It was already after nine. Liz pushed the speed limit driving through Watertown and Waltham even though she knew local cops almost always set speed traps. Her brain was numb, but it didn't completely smother her sense of dread. Glenn was going to be furious. Liz slammed her hand on the steering wheel—why had Glenn picked Wednesday night for this dinner? Glenn knew Wednesday was her worst day of the week!

At the house Glenn's car was the only one in the driveway. Liz knocked at the front door, not daring to use her own key. When Glenn opened it, Liz felt her heart stop in cold fear.

"Did you get your work done?" Glenn asked snidely when they were both inside.

"Glenn, I'm sorry. I'm so sorry," Liz said, powerless against her tears. "I completely forgot dinner."

"Is that supposed to make me feel better?" Glenn snapped. She walked away until she stood on the far side of the room.

"I guess I know the truth now," Glenn said in a voice colder than Liz had ever heard her use. "If I had any doubts before, I certainly don't now. You care far more about your precious work than you do about me." She turned away.

"That's not true! I'm sorry, Glenn. I feel terrible—"

Glenn whirled around. "You feel terrible? How do you think I felt all night, sitting here with Diana and Joyce, waiting for you? When you never showed up, they were the ones making excuses for you. Diana even called the Boston police to see if there had been any bad traffic accidents!"

Liz hung her head, pained beyond words.

"This is just too typical, Liz."

"Typical?" Liz repeated, not understanding.

Glenn stood across the room, her arms folded on her chest. There was no sympathy in her eyes or in her voice. "Of what's important to you. And of what's not. I'm not your priority. This relationship is not your priority. For the last six weeks all you have cared about is school. I can't take it, Liz. I won't be involved with someone who won't be involved with me."

"That's not true," Liz whispered hoarsely. Horrible fear was spreading through her. "What do you want from me?" she asked desperately.

Glenn threw her hands into the air. "I want you not to have to ask that question. I want you to know how to value a relationship. I feel like I never see you. And when I do, you're not really there. Do you ever turn off from school, Liz? I know you have a lot of work to do, but it's getting harder and harder for me to believe that's not just your excuse for holding back from me!"

Liz just stared.

Glenn went on, "You never talk to me, Liz. We have to be able to talk about hard things when they come up. I want you to tell me—to yell at me if you have to—about why it's so hard for you to take my money, or just to let me buy things for you! I want you to talk to me about why you don't want to live together. For god's sake, I want you to be able to talk to me about Chris! But, oh no, when anything the least bit threatening comes up, you always find the most clever ways of avoiding the subject. You told me a long time ago that you would talk to me, that you would tell me anything I wanted to know about you, Liz. What happened to that promise?"

"I guess it's not as easy as I thought it would be," Liz replied, hardly knowing what she was saying. Something was shattering inside her as she suffered Glenn's ice-hard glare. When Glenn turned away—again—Liz suddenly felt more angry than afraid.

"So everything's my fault? I'm sorry I've been such a problem for you," she said, thickly sarcastic.

She grew angrier. If it was over—it seemed whatever they had was over—she wasn't through.

"Don't make it sound so easy, Glenn. It's not that easy to talk." When Glenn refused to say anything, Liz exclaimed, "If you think it's so goddamned easy to tell someone what you're feeling, why don't you tell your mother how lousy you feel about your relationship?"

Glenn whirled around, white with rage. "I tried, Liz. At least I tried to talk to my mother and my father."

"One chance—is that all people get with you? Well I'm glad to know now." Blind with fury and pain, Liz turned and headed for the door. Glenn didn't say a word to stop her.

Liz reached her car. Inside, she turned the motor on. Then she sat there, not moving only because she had no idea where to go. Reluctantly, she turned the car off. More slowly, she got out of the car and went back to the door, this time letting herself in. Glenn hadn't moved.

"We need to start over," Liz said softly.

Glenn shrugged miserably. "Which—our whole relationship, or this night?"

"This night," Liz said, walking closer. She saw that Glenn was crying again.

"Were Diana and Joyce angry?" she asked, struggling to stay calm.

"Of course not." Glenn started to say something else but then broke off in new sobs.

Liz moved a little closer. She wanted to touch Glenn, but she felt too frightened. As Glenn's sobs became louder, Liz grew less certain what to do.

"Glenn, do you want me to leave?" she asked, terrified what she would do if Glenn said yes.

"No."

Liz went to the sofa and sat down. Glenn remained standing near the dining room table. Liz looked down at her hands, pressing them gently into each other. As the minutes passed, when Glenn still wouldn't look at her, Liz began to wonder if it wouldn't be easier if she did just leave.

"Glenn," she said, standing and walking closer. "Please, Glenn, talk to me."

Glenn laughed shortly; Liz guessed what she was thinking —that her words sounded too ironic. She moved closer and put one hand tentatively on Glenn's waist. Glenn didn't move away.

Finally Glenn said, "I'm hurt right now, Liz. I'm just really hurt. About dinner. About all the things I've thought about you—about us—tonight."

They went to the sofa, physically close, at least for the moment.

"What I said before," Glenn started, "I'm sorry for the way I blurted everything out." She took a deep breath. "But I can't apologize for what I said. It's how I feel—or how I've felt, anyway. I love you, Liz. I love you in ways that frighten and unnerve me because sometimes when I look at you, I have this feeling I don't even know you and I just can't understand how I can love someone so much whom I don't even know."

Liz looked down, feeling a rise of new panic.

"Sorry. I'm exaggerating again," Glenn said softly. "But I don't know how else to say what I'm thinking."

Glenn was calming down. Liz felt it even as she felt herself sinking further into a dizzying swell of confusion and dread. Something inside was spinning wildly out of control. Glenn drew her close, but Liz felt only the distance between them.

"Liz, are you all right?" Glenn asked after several minutes had passed.

"I don't think so."

Liz suffered the silent moments passing, certain she was disappointing Glenn again.

"You know how I am," Glenn said in a tone of gentle apology. "I overreact. If I'm thinking something, I have to say it."

And you know how I am, Liz thought, not listening to whatever else Glenn was saying—so why is it okay for you to be how you are, and I have to change?

"Okay?" Glenn said.

"What?" Liz asked, abruptly looking at her.

"Let's go upstairs."

Glenn took her hand. Upstairs, Liz dressed for bed mechanically. Then Glenn came to her and unbuttoned her thin flannel shirt, slipping it off. Liz felt Glenn's fingers tugging at her underwear, wanting her to remove them. Underneath the covers Glenn slid across the bed to hold her. Liz pressed her head into Glenn's bare shoulder.

The roar of emotion swelled thunderously in her ears. Liz trembled violently, lost in the chaos of feelings she couldn't name. There was nothing but feeling scared, shaking in Glenn's arms.

"What is it, Liz?"

"I'm just so scared," Liz whispered, reluctantly letting her eyes move to Glenn's.

Liz saw no fear in Glenn's eyes, but her own terror was not eased. There was still the void inside herself. There was still the distance between them.

Glenn's eyes held her, more powerfully than her arms. Liz looked into them, startled when she felt herself moving beyond fear.

Something was opening, something she hadn't known could be there—some place for her and Glenn to be together. In the quiet of the room, in the certainty of the love she saw in Glenn's eyes, Liz let herself move into it.

Chapter Thirteen

"Laura asked about you again today," Glenn said.

Liz turned from the stereo where she had just switched records. "Oh? What did she say?"

"She wanted to know whether we could all get together for lunch sometime. She hadn't said anything for a month—I was hoping she had given up the idea. But today she asked whether I still see you. I admitted I do." Glenn shook her head uncertainly. "I think Laura may know a lot more about my life than I'd be comfortable having her know."

Liz walked over to the sofa. "Laura likes you. She wouldn't say anything to anyone, even if she does know or suspect that you're a lesbian."

"You never told Laura about yourself, did you?" Glenn asked.

"No. For a long time I think she wanted to know more about my personal life. One time she mentioned two gay guys who are friends of hers. I wondered if she wasn't hinting then that I should feel free to talk if I wanted to."

Liz leaned against Glenn, enjoying the sound of Stevie Nicks' voice.

"I was thinking about Thanksgiving today," Glenn said.

"Thanksgiving? What month is it, anyway?"

"It's November. Thanksgiving isn't for three more weeks, but I was thinking about cooking dinner here. We could invite

Alice and any of your other friends. And of course, Pamela and Diana and Joyce."

Liz felt herself stiffen. "Do you really think Diana and Joyce would come—after what happened the last time we planned a dinner?" she said, trying to joke. The botched dinner was weeks in the past; Liz had seen Diana and Joyce twice since then. Though she knew all had been forgiven— that Diana and Joyce had never truly been angry with her— instantly she dreaded the thought of another dinner.

———

Liz looked over her shoulder when she heard the apartment door open the next night. "Hello," she said, glad Alice was home.

"Hi," Alice answered.

"Busy night at the club?" Liz asked. Alice had recently returned to working at the health club, her part-time job through the fall and winter.

"Not bad. Is Glenn here?"

"No."

"Two nights apart in two weeks," Alice mumbled sarcastically, distracted as she leafed through her share of the day's mail. She looked up from the counter. "I sure hope things are okay between you two."

Liz threw a pillow, but Alice ignored it. "Things are great. Oh, I wanted to ask you, do you have any plans yet for Thanksgiving? Glenn wants to have dinner at her house. It'd be great if you could come."

Alice shrugged noncommittally. "Thanksgiving—that falls on a Thursday this year, doesn't it?"

Liz indulged her with a laugh. "This year and every year. I talked to Jeanne earlier tonight. She's going to come."

Alice, already across the living room and disappearing down the hall, didn't reply.

Liz picked up the textbook she had abandoned when Alice came home. She found her place, but database design concepts no longer held much interest for her. Something in Alice's coolness bothered her. Immediately, Liz felt defensive, worried that Alice was angry with her again. But they had had dinner together last week. And she had seen Alice at soccer on Tuesday nights the last few weeks. Well, she had made it to soccer twice recently, anyway.

Alice came back into the living room. She had changed out of her work clothes into baggy gray sweat pants, holes at the knees, and an extra-large t-shirt. She leapt lightly to the chinning bar which spanned the entrance to the hallway and began doing pull-ups. Liz counted fifteen before Alice dropped to the floor, breathing hard. Ten was usually her limit.

"Good job," Liz said, admiringly. "Feeling especially strong tonight?"

Alice sat down on the floor in the living room, answering only, "No." In a brighter voice, she said, "So, things really are okay with Glenn now?"

Liz closed her textbook. "Yes. Much better. Thanks again for listening to me when things were so crazy a few weeks ago. I thought I was going to lose my mind. But I guess I'm not telling you anything."

"Hey, what are friends for?" Alice asked flatly.

"It seems funny now," Liz continued. "I mean, it's not always easy to talk to Glenn, but I'm not as afraid to try as I used to be. Before, I think I always imagined the worst, that if Glenn and I talked about our problems, they would seem so much bigger than they really were—so it was better not to mention them. The funny thing is, it seems like it's just the opposite. Not that it's really as easy as all that," she ended, knowing she had oversimplified what had changed for her and Glenn.

"Well there's really just one thing I want to know," Alice said in a harder voice. "When do you plan to tell me you're moving out? Am I going to come home someday and find a note on the counter—'By the way, Alice, I'm living with Glenn now. It's been fun.'—Jesus, Liz, you'd probably leave your final rent check and pat yourself on the back for being oh so incredibly responsible!"

Liz stared in disbelief. "What's going on?" she asked in a whisper.

"That's what I'd like to know!" Alice returned. "The writing's on the wall, Liz. I'm not blind. Glenn is your world now. You and I haven't spent any time together all fall except for those occasional fluky nights when we both end up here. And when, besides at soccer, have you seen Jeanne for the last three months? You've abandoned your friends, Liz, and let me say—just for the record—that that is not all right with me!"

"I knew you were mad at me," Liz continued in the same low voice. "Do you think I haven't missed seeing you?"

"That'd be a little hard for me to tell, quite honestly."

"I have. God, I have, Alice. I've practically gone crazy trying to hold everything together. You may have noticed I didn't do such a great job of that. Three weeks ago I was terrified Glenn and I were going to break up. Now you're telling me I've screwed up our friendship."

Alice scowled. "No. I'm not saying that. I'm just mad, Liz. I don't want to become part of the 'painful past' you leave behind when you go waltzing off into marital bliss with Glenn, that's all."

"I'm not going anywhere!" Liz insisted. "Okay, so we have talked about living together. Okay, so maybe we will someday. But Alice, we haven't made that decision. And whenever and however that happens, I don't intend for that to interfere with your and my friendship!"

Alice stared hard at her. "Well then you'd better figure out what you're going to do about that, because right now I don't feel like I happen to have much of a place in your life."

Alice stood up and left the room. Liz watched her retreating figure until only the emptiness of the hallway remained in view. She hesitated one moment, then followed her.

The door of the bedroom was ajar; Liz had expected to find it closed. Alice stood between her bed and the dresser, half turned away. Liz couldn't tell whether she was crying.

"This conversation isn't over," Liz said softly.

Alice just shrugged.

Liz stepped into the room. "Believe me, Alice, I've missed you. I haven't liked how crazy my life's been. The only thing that's kept me going was thinking it couldn't go on forever like it was."

Alice didn't respond.

"Please, Alice, talk to me!"

Alice barely turned. Her mouth was twisted in a pained expression; rare emotion showed in her eyes. "I'm sorry I blew up just now," she said. "I don't even know where that came from. I guess I've just been thinking that sooner or later things between us would go back to how they were last year—hanging out here nights, going out to the bar once in a while. Then I realized I was an idiot for thinking that." Alice took a deep breath. "I'm just not sure about you, Liz. I feel afraid that you either are, or are going to be, so absorbed with Glenn, with getting closer to her and making whatever plans you make for the future, that you're not going to realize you need to take care of your other friendships."

Alice continued before Liz managed to respond. "Come on, I didn't need to ask how things are between you and Glenn. It's obvious they're great. You're happier than you've been since I've known you. I'm glad Glenn makes you happy." Alice's eyes flickered away. "Sometimes I've wished I could make you happy. You should be happy. I just don't want to be left behind," she ended, still subdued.

Liz met Alice's eyes when she looked up, feeling connected, yet not grasping everything Alice had just told her. But she had heard. For all of their teasing and joking through this last year, not everything had been in jest. Behind Alice, Liz saw her bed. One time they had slept together there—once, they had made love. Until now, that was the only strain their friendship had ever suffered.

Liz walked over and put her arms around Alice. Alice returned her tight embrace. "Then you're going to have to help me," Liz said. "You're going to have to tell me if I start acting like a jerk, okay?"

Alice pulled her tighter. Liz was startled by the urgency she felt in Alice's hug. Then Alice stepped back, brushing her lips lightly across Liz's cheek. "If?" she asked, familiar laughter moving into her eyes, a wry smile beginning to crease the corners of her mouth. "Start?" she added in the same ironic tone.

Liz just shook her, mockingly ferocious.

❀

Thursday, Thanksgiving morning, Liz was up early to help Glenn with the cooking. The day was unusually warm; by noon the outside temperature peaked at sixty-five degrees. Throughout the morning and early afternoon mild winds blew steadily. Sudden gusts would draw white caps on the lake and send clouds speeding across the sky. In all ways the weather was so uncharacteristic that Liz wondered whether it signaled imminent drastic change.

Alice and Jeanne were the first to arrive. Neither was seeing anyone else at the moment and they had jokingly agreed to be each other's date.

Then Pamela arrived, and not long afterwards Diana and Joyce appeared at the door. Liz flushed with pleasure when Diana pulled her close and kissed her cheek. Diana kept one arm around her as they walked in to join the others in the living room.

Liz had waited weeks for Alice to have this opportunity to meet Diana. Alice, Liz knew perfectly well, had never believed her accounts of Diana's beauty. She was pleased when Alice and Diana hit it off immediately. It started when Alice told the story of a woman who had come to the health club where she worked, hoping to lose a few pounds before Thanksgiving. She had shown up for the first time the day before.

"What did you tell her?" Diana asked.

"Oh, I told her it would be no problem," Alice said in the dry, deadpan tone of voice which Liz knew Alice used when she was setting something up. "But I did suggest that she might want to stop at the snack bar before starting her workout. That was the last I saw of her."

Diana burst out laughing. She went on to tell the story of her own one and only visit to a health club. Liz glanced at Diana's lean physique; she guessed that in addition to her other impressive qualities, Diana was also probably a natural athlete.

By the time dinner ended and the cluttered table was abandoned for the greater space in the living room, everyone seemed to be feeling well-satisfied. "Well, what shall we talk about?" Pamela asked when several seconds passed and no one spoke.

"I read an interesting article the other day," Jeanne said.

Hearing these words, so familiar from their soccer post-game gatherings, Liz and Alice looked at each other, their faces frozen with panic. Liz knew Jeanne could be starting in on anything from the evils of global pollution to the timely question of why baseball was regaining national popularity. Alice and Liz broke out laughing.

Jeanne looked at them and frowned, but said, "It was in the *Wall Street Journal,* of all places, and what it said, basically, was that women have to create structures—social structures —out of their own strengths and not content themselves with mimicking male structures. And when that happens, they truly could have a power to be reckoned with—"

"By whom?" Pamela asked, interrupting.

Jeanne shrugged. "The issue wasn't confrontation; the article gave an argument for an alternative social organization. A powerful alternative, strong in its own right, but not created

166

out of any need to compete. In fact the article implied that competition would not be endemic to any organization created by women, at least not as it is known among men."

"I read the same article," Diana said. "At first I thought the author—whose sexual identity was disguised by the use of initials—was taking pot shots at existing women's groups, at business networking organizations, primarily, which have grown up in major cities around the country. But he, or she, wasn't. It really was about tapping into greater strengths which are not uniquely female, but which are predominantly female and using those strengths to build new, viable social structures."

"None of which is a new thought," Joyce said.

"No. But for the *Wall Street Journal?*" Diana said. The group laughed.

"It made me think about some different things," Jeanne said. "I forget sometimes that so much in this world was created by men—and women—and that much of what exists might have been created otherwise. Our social structures are products of our minds and our hands. It's easy to forget that, to assume that what is must be, and that it is not for us to question."

"We have a rebel in our midst," Pamela said softly.

Liz laughed and said, "No. Only one who dares to imagine that this world might improve."

Pamela replied, "Just as I said, a rebel. Jeanne," she continued, "are you saying that our problems lie wholly in our limited imaginations—that freedom is ours for the asking?"

"No. Even I don't think it's that simple. But what I do think is that we have more knots than we realize in our minds—individually and as a society—which prevent us from seeking what we want and need. We have to understand how we handicap ourselves, and of course, then stop doing so."

"For example?" Alice asked.

"Slavery," Diana replied without hesitating. "There was a time when no one seriously questioned the morality of slave ownership. Of course no one was going to do anything about it until it was brought into question. But I think that's almost too obvious for what you're getting at, isn't it, Jeanne?"

"It's the same idea. Another example would be individuals who never question their religious training even after they become adults and after they've grown to feel dissatisfied by their church's dogma. I'm not dumping on religions. But I am

167

dumping on people who cling to a faith unquestioned, who refuse to trust the power of their own minds to discover answers. Some people can live on a simple faith. Most people encounter serious gaps when it comes to reconciling their lives with what their religion teaches. And to defer to the bland doctrine of some remote theology rather than to exercise the fullness of one's own mind, well, that to me is akin to willfully tying one's mind in knots."

"Recognizing the knots isn't always easy. How do you do that?" Liz asked.

"You pay attention," Jeanne said.

Glenn spoke for the first time, returning to the original thrust of this conversation, fantasizing on what form an alternative women's organization might take. Talk became animated as others joined in. Liz and Alice exchanged glances more than once: the night was identical to many when they had sat together with their team after games, the only difference, in this group no one wore a grass-stained shirt.

It was late when the party broke up. Liz stood with Glenn and cast a long, speculative look towards the kitchen. The dirty dishes could wait until morning.

———

Friday was a quiet day. The weather had turned suddenly cold; neither Liz nor Glenn had any desire to go out. They cleaned the house, talked, fired up the wood stove, then sat in the warmth of the living room.

All day Liz had thought more about what Jeanne had said the night before. She marveled at how often she came away from discussions with Jeanne thinking harder, and differently, about things she had never wondered about before. Jeanne had touched something in her when she spoke of minds tied in knots. Lately, Liz had felt acutely her inner boundaries. She sensed they were there, but she had no idea how to get past them.

"Sometimes," she said to Glenn, "I think all of my worrying about school, about money, about when we should live together, it's all just a big smoke screen."

Glenn looked at her curiously.

"It's easy to focus on those things. Not that they aren't important, because they are. But being preoccupied with them keeps me from looking at other things, things that might be more important."

"I believe I said the same to you the last time we talked about living together. As I recall, you did not take kindly to the idea." Glenn paused. "So what do you think is behind your smoke screen?"

Liz sighed deeply. "I don't know. I just feel myself holding back, not giving as much as I know I have it in me to give."

"You have a lot to give, Liz, and you do give a lot. But that's not what this is all about."

Liz smiled wryly. "What is it all about? I've been waiting for someone to tell me."

"It's about giving it all. You think you can get away with giving bits and pieces of yourself, and you probably could. But not with the people who matter most to you."

Liz looked down. "Alice said something like that to me recently."

"Liz," Glenn said slowly, "were you and Alice—"

"Ever lovers?"

Glenn nodded.

"No. We slept together once. I'm not even sure why."

"Alice is a very attractive woman."

Liz was quiet. She didn't tell Glenn that Alice's physical appearance was only part of her attraction; she didn't add that Alice had an extraordinary ability to seduce through her touch.

"Liz," Glenn said, "could you tell me again about your relationship with Chris?"

"I've told you everything before," Liz replied, knowing this answer would get her nowhere.

"Tell me again. I've forgotten."

Liz almost didn't care, though when she had started this conversation, her intention had not been to talk about Chris.

Glenn was speaking. "So, when Chris came to you the first time and told you that she was sleeping with—who was it?—and basically rewrote all of the rules in your relationship, you didn't see how that hurt you?"

"Well, I didn't like it, if that's what you're getting at. At the time I didn't feel I had any choice but to accept her conditions if I had any hope of her coming back to me."

"And you had that hope?"

"Yes. We had been through so much that was bad. I wanted to salvage something of what was good."

Glenn's expression became thoughtful. "I wonder if you can ever do that."

169

"Of course you can," Liz nearly snapped. "People do it all the time." Or so she had always believed.

"Yet, later, when Chris did come back, you didn't want her."

"I didn't want her, that's true. I hated her. I know that now. I didn't know that then."

"Liz, if you were so unhappy, why didn't you do something different—like leave her?"

"I didn't want Chris to know that she had hurt me," Liz said quietly. "I pretended that I didn't care. She had made a farce of our relationship. I wanted to do the same. I didn't love her any more, but I acted as if I did."

"So you knowingly stayed in a situation that was hurting you just so you could hurl your spears of disdain towards Chris? A little masochistic, don't you think?"

Liz closed her eyes and felt the room begin to spin. Glenn wasn't mincing words tonight. Out of nowhere Liz heard a remote voice whining, saying, "You're a fool, Liz, everyone knows it."

Liz felt Glenn rubbing her neck gently. "Why do you keep coming back to this?" she asked. She spoke slowly and resolutely, determined to eradicate the other voice by the strength of her own.

"It seems only too obvious. There's some part of this that still bothers you very much."

With quiet emphasis on each word, Liz said, "I'll be okay. I will get over this. Time will pass, and I will get through it."

"It's been two years, Liz. Don't you think you're taking the long road home?"

"I'm taking my road."

Glenn laughed. "You know, it's funny. You and I are so different. With me, my anxiety and fears tend to be right up front. When they're there, you can't miss them. But if I can get through them, then I'm past them. You're much more easy-going on the surface, but underneath, your fears are great and they do hold you back. They're harder to unravel because they stay hidden."

"Is that what you think?"

"It's what I know."

"I don't understand," Liz said. "Every time we have one of these conversations we end up back at Chris. That part of my life is over. I don't understand why you keep going back to it."

Glenn laughed easily. "Is any part of our life ever over? The events may stop, but our feelings about those events live on. Like it or not, those feelings influence us." Glenn paused. "All right, I confess—I think you still want something from Chris. I'm curious to know what that is."

Liz frowned. Of all the things she had thought about Chris since their breakup, she had never thought this.

Glenn laughed when she saw Liz perplexed. She brushed her hair away from her neck and kissed her. "I love you, you know I do."

Liz smiled and nodded. Leaning closer, she touched her lips to Glenn's.

Chapter Fourteen

Liz slipped quietly out of bed. She took her blue jeans and thick sweatshirt from the hook on the door, then went to the bathroom to dress.

Downstairs, she wrapped a blanket around herself while she sat at the kitchen table. It was early—just seven o'clock—early especially for a Saturday and a vacation day. It was January. She was still on her break between semesters.

Liz sipped from her cup of hot water. Grinding coffee beans would be sure to wake Glenn and it was too early for that. She sat at the table and looked through the windows to the wintry scene of the lake below.

January—it was hard to believe it was already a new year. She and Glenn had both been back from visits with their families for more than a week. Now she only had one more week of vacation left before school started again.

Since school had ended in December, she had virtually been living here with Glenn. It wasn't a question any longer whether she would live with Glenn. The only question was when she would move out of the apartment. But that was still a question. Liz frowned, hating the thought of telling Alice. It was silly—but she didn't want things to change between them. Yet things already had changed. Between her spending so much time here and Alice working long hours at her two jobs, they had hardly seen each other for all of this last month.

The last time they had had dinner together was weeks ago—before Christmas. Alice had been subdued that night, Liz remembered. Just tired, Alice had said; but that night she had admitted she sometimes still felt jealous of Glenn. Liz smiled sadly, remembering what Alice had said about her jealousy: "It's not fair, but what in life is fair?" Alice had told her she loved her. Liz took a deep breath, wishing it were as easy for her to tell Alice how much she loved her. Oh, she had said the words—but only after Alice had said them first.

Liz stood up and walked to the sliding glass doors. She leaned against the pane of cold glass. The lake was a frozen span of white down below. Through the bare trees she saw the nearest neighbor's yard and the space they had cleared on the ice for skating.

She thought of what had her up so early on this cold winter's morning, trying to feel amused at the irony—that as soon as she had told herself this was the one thing she could never tell Glenn, she knew it was the one thing she had to tell her.

––––––

"You're quiet tonight," Glenn said.

"Am I—" Liz started to say, "I guess I am." She stood up and walked to the windows in the kitchen.

Glenn waited a moment. "Liz, if you walk into that kitchen one more time—what is it? Is there something out there you're looking at?"

Liz turned and smiled. "No. It's not out there." She came back into the living room. "I have something I want to tell you. But every time I think I'm going to say it, I get up and go look outside instead."

"What is it?"

Liz paced three steps. "It's a story, really. But before I start, you have to promise me that you'll just let me tell it, no matter how long it takes or how muddled it sounds while I'm telling it."

Glenn's expression softened. "I can promise that."

Liz turned and paced back the same three steps. "I want to tell you what the ending is about first, just in case I chicken out before I get there. That way, you can know whether I've really told everything." She stopped.

"Okay," Glenn said.

"The ending's about how I was able to leave Syracuse— why I left when I did."

Already Liz felt unable to look at Glenn. She felt heat rising in her body—anxiety; she could not keep her voice steady.

"One of the things I wonder about a lot is change," she started. She looked at Glenn, safe with this for the moment. "Do you think people can really change?"

Glenn looked puzzled. "In what way?"

"How they are, I guess. I just wonder, if you know you've been a certain way, how can you be sure you won't get to be that way again, assuming you know you don't want to be that way?"

Glenn didn't say anything.

Liz sighed heavily. "I guess I should just say it. I've tried to tell you parts of this before, about how awful I felt when I was with Chris. I don't think I've ever said it right."

"Tell me now," Glenn said softly.

Liz shrugged and paced again, then flopped down in the chair at the end of the sofa.

"Things got to be so horrible between us. I never saw the moment when I stopped loving Chris. One day it was just different. I was doing and saying the same things I had for who knows how long. But it was different. My words were calculated, and every action was deliberate—staged, almost."

Liz looked at Glenn. "I should have left then. That's so clear to me now. But at the time I felt this crazy, intoxicating feeling, knowing it was so easy to fool Chris about how I felt. Every kindness was a mockery—every word I said to her was false. I got so lost in my own power to deceive that I couldn't see what I was doing to myself."

Liz stared blankly straight ahead. "I didn't know any other lesbians then. I wasn't out to any of my straight friends. The worse things got with Chris, the more I pulled away from people. First, I didn't want to tell anyone I was a lesbian; then, by the time I didn't care about that, I just felt so ashamed of myself that I wouldn't have told anyone anything, even if there had been anyone to tell."

"Why ashamed?" Glenn asked.

"Why ashamed?" Liz repeated. She laughed shortly. "I felt ashamed, I think, because I had chosen to love someone who could hurt me so much. I felt pretty stupid—like it was my fault that I was hurt, that I should have been able to choose someone who would love me better. I guess blaming myself was easier than blaming Chris."

Liz took a deep breath, worried that it still wasn't coming out right. "Things never were one way or the other between us. We went back and forth a thousand times, about whether we would be lovers, whether we—Chris, that is—would be monogamous, or whether we would just be the roommates we were telling the world we were. When Chris first started staying away at night, I thought I would lose my mind. Then, when she would come back, I never knew how things would be. I didn't know what to do. I knew I had wanted her, a life with her, once. I guess I clung to that long past when it was healthy for me—or us—to think that was possible.

"I felt so trapped," Liz said wearily. "I didn't know how to leave. I kept trying to go along with how Chris wanted things to be because I didn't know what else to do. Anything to keep the peace with her was worth something. I learned to hate her. But I hated myself more. I think part of why I stayed with her was because I knew it was the worst possible thing I could do for myself—and by then all I wanted was to hurt myself more.

"Through all of this I somehow managed to hold a job and apply to graduate school at BU. I was accepted. Chris and I did move to separate apartments. I kept thinking that all I had to do was make it until the summer, then I could move to Boston."

Liz stopped. The words were flowing, but in one form or another she had told nearly this much before. It was the other she had never said.

"But you didn't stay until summer," Glenn prompted softly.

"No." Liz took a deep breath. "I left in February. By then I had been living by myself for five months. I had hoped that as soon as I was on my own, I'd be all right again. Well, that didn't happen. Chris and I still saw each other. I tried to see other friends, but I just felt so awful when I did. It was as if there was nothing good left inside me and I had to make sure no one saw that. So, when I'd go out with other people we'd talk about their lives. I wouldn't say anything about myself. Everything was superficial. But by then, I thought that's just how I was, that there really wasn't anything else to me. I had no idea how much anger and pain—and guilt—I had inside me. You talk about someone who needed therapy," Liz said, trying to speak lightly.

Glenn returned half a smile.

"So, I called Chris one night. I had had a really lousy day at work. I didn't want to be alone. All I wanted was to go out and get something to eat. When I called, Chris, in her own infuriating way, made it clear there was someone new in her life. It was hardly the first time. But this time I couldn't take it.

"I guess I lost it," Liz said softly. "It felt like one more slap in the face, one more rejection, one more time that I had to live by her rules. I went out to my car and I just started driving. I left the city and found back country roads." Liz paused. "It had rained that day. It was cold, but not icy. I just kept driving, driving fast, hating Chris and myself and everything else I could think of. I don't know what I wanted to do," she said quietly, then stopped.

Glenn didn't say a word.

"I was driving on this straight stretch; there was a bend up ahead. By then I was going really fast. I barely slowed for the curve. When I came around it there was this car in front of me. It had pulled onto the road and it had stopped." Liz hesitated. "I didn't hit it. But I did have a wreck. I wrecked my car."

Glenn was on the chair beside her. "Were you hurt?" she asked.

Liz shook her head no.

"Liz, were you trying to kill yourself?"

Liz clutched her head and broke into tears. "I don't know. I just didn't care any more. I honestly don't know what I was trying to do." She couldn't say another word.

Glenn held her tightly while tears streamed from her eyes. Liz thought they would never stop. But they did; Glenn promised they would. Liz hardly knew what Glenn said to her—she remembered hearing only gentle words of comfort, words of concern.

Later, when she could talk, she said, "When I think about everything that happened, sometimes I still feel I have no right to be in a relationship, that I shouldn't trust myself and that no one should trust me." She looked at Glenn, but Glenn only smiled and brushed the tears on her cheeks.

"If I thought there was any chance that I could hurt you, I don't know, I couldn't take that," she added.

Glenn held her tighter. "It takes two, Liz. I won't let you hurt me. I'll try not to let you hurt yourself. But you wouldn't. Look at how much you've learned since then."

Liz looked down. "I'm not sure anyone ever knows enough."

"Maybe not. We have to do the best we can."

Liz pressed her head against Glenn's shoulder. She felt completely drained. Bitterness was still strong inside her, but maybe not as strong as it had once been. Glenn was still with her. Tonight nothing mattered more than that.

❀

Liz closed the apartment door quietly behind her. She didn't hear any sounds inside—Alice probably wasn't up yet. In the living room she stopped to turn up the heat then went to her own room.

This morning she and Alice were going to the health club where Alice worked part-time. Alice had promised to teach her what she knew about lifting weights.

In her chest of drawers Liz found shorts and a t-shirt—clothes she hadn't needed for months. She opened her closet, looking for tennis shoes. The closet appeared barren. Liz looked through it, surprised to find it so empty; but on one trip or another she had moved nearly all of her winter clothes to Glenn's. All that remained here were summer clothes and the few skirts and dresses she rarely wore.

Turning, Liz glanced around. There was an emptiness in the room—it was empty of her presence, anyway. Oh, the prints on the walls were still there: the one of Provincetown harbor, sailing masts rising high above small and large boats, the washed-out gray of houses and buildings on shore; and the one of five doors, each painted a different color. Liz went to her dresser to look for the photo of the soccer team taken last fall. She had intended to frame it months ago.

Liz looked around the room again, feeling its vacantness, yet feeling the claim it still made on her, that she should return and live here. But she knew she would never do that. Liz left her bedroom and walked down the hall.

"I thought we were going to pump some iron today," she said, entering Alice's bedroom after hearing Alice's groggy reply to her knock.

"We are. Come here, you crazy woman," Alice said, still more asleep than awake.

Liz walked over to the bed. When she was close, Alice reached for her hand then pulled her towards the bed. Liz fell easily alongside her. "What time is it?" Alice asked.

"Eight-thirty."

"Ahh!" Alice cried. "The club doesn't even open until eleven."

"Good. Let's go get something to eat."

They went out to breakfast, then on to the health club. Throughout the morning Liz thought about what she needed to tell Alice today. For days she had been rehearsing the words. Last night, worried that she still wouldn't say everything right, she had written Alice a card. Now she wondered whether that had been the right thing to do.

The lines of love and friendship, Liz thought, repeating the words while Alice led her from one piece of equipment to another. As the minutes passed, while her body worked the machines Alice had chosen for her, she began to think how futile her impulse had been to try to draw some box around her feelings, to try to say to Alice, *I love you, I want our friendship to be this*. She could say the words, and she might even believe for one moment or longer they were true; but they were not true. She could not, now or ever, draw a line around any love and say, I want to hold this, I will keep this forever.

"You're a lot stronger than I thought you were, Edwards," Alice said, couching new insult under the guise of a compliment. They left the Nautilus room and went to the room with the stationary bicycles—torture chambers, Liz was beginning to think. "I thought you'd be crying for mercy long before now," Alice added.

"From this?" Liz replied. "This feels like a day at the beach."

They entered a room which held half a dozen bicycles. Alice adjusted the tension on two of the units. She said, "Hold it at fifteen miles per hour for fifteen minutes. We'll see if you can still walk after that."

Liz and Alice climbed onto their separate frames.

For the first four minutes Liz spun the pedals easily. After that her legs began to feel heavy with fatigue. She gripped the handles and kept her eyes riveted on the flashing digits on the monitor at the base of the frame. All that kept her going was Alice's promise that after this they would end the day in the sauna.

The spinning back wheels filled the air with a whirring sound. Disco music played in the adjacent room. Liz looked at the red numbers flashing on the bicycle's small box: six minutes gone, nearly seven.

Let it go, Edwards, she whispered—let go of the line.

She pushed harder at the pedals, repeating what she had told herself earlier: the love that is true is the love that bursts and comes to life in the present.

Liz looked up to stare at the far wall. She heard other words echoing silently: the past does not bind you and the future promises nothing.

From somewhere deep inside Liz felt new strength flooding her body. She pushed the pedals furiously. She did love Alice, and she would show Alice that love each day they were together. She didn't need the artificial expression of a card or mere words to prove what she felt in her heart.

"How you doing over there?" Alice called out.

"I'm doing great," Liz replied, smiling wide. The eight changed to nine. Six minutes to go. Her legs drove the pedals; her brain, lungs, and heart drove her legs. Keep it strong, she whispered, keep it strong.

The heat of the sauna was penetrating, soothing. Liz used her towel to wipe beads of sweat from her brow. Alice, sitting next to her, exhaled a tired groan. Liz shared the feeling she heard in Alice's sigh: relief at being able simply to sit; the pure pleasure of feeling heat soaking into her.

"Great workout today," Alice said. "I bet you'll feel it tomorrow."

"Maybe," Liz answered flatly.

"Hey, Liz," Alice flashed a sardonic expression, "don't try and fool me. I know you too well for that."

Liz only smiled, suddenly too aware of the knot in her stomach to manage a response. She had put off telling Alice all day; she couldn't put it off any longer.

"Then you probably know how much I don't want to say what I'm going to say," she said, noticeably subdued.

"What? That you're finally moving out? God, Edwards, don't you think it's about time?"

"How'd you know what I was going to say?" Liz demanded, startled past her dejection.

Alice waited until Liz looked at her. "Liz, contrary to your deeply cherished opinion, I'm not an idiot. So when's moving day?"

Liz stared, stung by feelings of gratitude and love that Alice was letting this happen so easily. "I don't know," she stumbled. "I figured you'd need some time to find someone else to move in."

Alice shrugged. "That shouldn't take long. The big adjustment's going to be learning all over again how to live with someone who's normal." Alice pretended to smack her forehead with the base of her hand. "God! I never thought I'd hear myself say that!"

Liz tried to scowl; she tried twisting her towel into a thin strand to snap at Alice. Hearing Alice laugh, Liz gave up her feeble attempt to retaliate and laughed with her.

❀

"Tomorrow's your last day of vacation," Glenn said to Liz late Saturday night. "Would you like to do anything special?"

"Yes," Liz said, knowing in an instant. "Let's go to Maine. It may be a little cold," she added in a voice that hinted it might be a lot more than a little cold.

They reached the town of Ogunquit just before noon "Where to now?" Glenn asked.

Liz pointed to a road up ahead. "Turn right there." Glenn did. Liz directed her up a hill and through a wooded residential section. When they emerged from the short stretch, the Atlantic Ocean lay in front of them, white surf pounding the rocky shore.

The day was unseasonably mild, which was all that allowed them to be outside for more than brief moments. Dressed in layers of sweaters and coats, hats and gloves, Liz carried an extra blanket as they began walking along the public footpath that stood between the rock-strewn shore and the waterfront homes.

"This is crazy!" Glenn exclaimed after a sudden gust of wind sent chills through them both. But the sun, which had vanished behind clouds momentarily, reappeared, and the air warmed.

Liz laughed. "It is nuts," she agreed. "It's usually freezing here even in summer."

With Liz still leading, they cautiously picked their way down a rocky path, avoiding sections still covered by patches of snow. Ahead of them, waves crashed explosively, sending white foam spewing. Liz looked to the distant edge of the shore wistfully, but today they needed to find a protected space for the few minutes they could stay out here, and not go to the end and play chicken with incoming waves as she would have had it been warmer.

They found a small niche, partially surrounded by rocks but still affording a view of the water. They sat close, huddled beneath the blanket. Liz leaned against the hard rock; she closed her eyes and inhaled deeply, loving the salt scent and the roar of the waves hitting rocks.

"It's beautiful here," Glenn said. "I've only ever been to Ogunquit Beach. I had no idea these rocks were even here."

Liz opened her eyes. "This is one of my favorite places in the world. When I first moved to Boston I came here all the time."

They both shivered and huddled closer when a cloud passed over the sun. Glenn said, "When your lips start turning blue, we're leaving, no matter what you say."

Liz saw the dark tinge already in Glenn's and knew they'd have to leave soon anyway.

"Oh," Liz exclaimed, interrupting her deep sigh to laugh shortly. "I remember coming here so many times. This was the one place where I knew I could come and feel good—happy—at least for a little while. No matter how awful I felt in Boston, I always felt better here—refreshed somehow. Sitting here, watching the water, I would tell myself this was the way I wanted to feel all the time. It was my fix, I guess. What's funny is that I didn't know until just now how much better I do feel all the time."

Glenn reached for her hand under the blanket. "What's different, do you think?"

"I don't know." Liz looked out over the blue sea then looked at Glenn. "Being with you is different. Have I told you lately that I'm madly in love with you?"

Glenn smiled.

The waves rolled thunderously, crashing continuously into shore, a soothing roar; Liz wished she could take it with her. But today—for once—it was all right just to leave.

"You're the one whose lips are purple," Liz said a few minutes later. She moved the blanket and stood up, then offered her hand to Glenn.

At the path Liz felt Glenn slip her arm around her. They walked quickly, chilled through now, racing to find warmth somewhere beyond the cold, windy shore.

Amy and her partner have spent the last nine years traveling the country searching for perfect weather. While visiting friends in Denver in 1988, they joined a basketball team and have lived there ever since. Amy graduated from the University of Pittsburgh with a degree in philosophy. She avoids working real jobs as much as possible, spending her time instead writing and bicycling the Colorado mountain passes. Born in Pittsburgh, Pennsylvania in 1956, Amy grew up living alongside the Allegheny River and dreams of someday living again in a house by a river.

spinsters book company

Spinsters Book Company was founded in 1978 to produce vital books for diverse women's communities. In 1986 we merged with Aunt Lute Books to become Spinsters/Aunt Lute. In 1990, the Aunt Lute Foundation became an independant non-profit publishing program.

Spinsters is committed to publishing works outside the scope of mainstream commercial publishers: books that not only name crucial issues in women's lives, but more importantly encourage change and growth; books that help to make the best in our lives more possible. We sponsor an annual Lesbian Fiction Contest for the best lesbian novel each year. And we are particularly interested in creative works by lesbians.

If you would like to know about other books we produce, or our Fiction Contest, write or phone us for a free catalogue. You can buy books directly from us. We can also supply you with the name of a bookstore closest to you that stocks our books. We accept phone orders with Visa or Mastercard.

Spinsters Book Company
P.O. Box 410687
San Francisco, CA 94141
415-558-9586

Other Books Available From Spinsters Book Company

Bittersweet, by Nevada Barr $9.95

Cancer in Two Voices, by Sandra Butler
and Barbara Rosenblum $12.95

Child of Her People, by Anne Cameron $8.95

The Journey, by Anne Cameron $9.95

Prisons That Could Not Hold, by Barbara Deming $7.95

High and Outside, by Linnea A. Due $8.95

Elise, by Claire Kensington $7.95

Modern Daughters and the Outlaw West,
by Melissa Kwasny $9.95

*The Lesbian Erotic Dance: Butch, Femme, Androgyny,
and Other Rhythms,* by JoAnn Loulan $12.95

Lesbian Passion: Loving Ourselves and Each Other,
by JoAnn Loulan $11.95

Lesbian Sex, by JoAnn Loulan $10.95

Look Me in the Eye: Old Women, Aging and Ageism,
by Barbara Macdonald with Cynthia Rich $6.50

Being Someone, by Ann MacLeod $9.95

All the Muscle You Need, by Diana McRae $8.95

Final Session, by Mary Morell $9.95

Considering Parenthood, by Cheri Pies $9.50

Coz, by Mary Pjerrou $9.95

We Say We Love Each Other,
by Minnie Bruce Pratt $5.95

Desert Years: Undreaming the American Dream,
by Cynthia Rich $7.95

Lesbians at Midlife: The Creative Transition,
ed. by Barbara Sang, Joyce Warshow
and Adrienne J. Smith $12.95

Thirteen Steps: An Empowerment Process for Women,
by Bonita L. Swan $8.95

Why Can't Sharon Kowalski Come Home?
by Karen Thompson and Julie Andrzejewski $10.95

Spinsters titles are available at your local booksellers, or by mail order through Spinsters Book Company (415) 558-9586. A free catalogue is available upon request.

Please include $1.50 for the first title ordered, and $ .50 for every title thereafter. California residents, please add 8.25% sales tax. Visa and Mastercard accepted.